KANSAS CITY, MO. PUBLIC LIBRARY

0 0001 5169267 0

MAIN

P9-DBI-785

DATE DUE

MAY 1 2 199

MAI OCT 1 2 1996

MAI DEC 1 3 1996

MAI AUG 2 9 199

OCT 1 7 1996

J 398.2 S764

Spooky stories for a
dark and stormy night /
c1994.

SPOOKY
STORIES
FOR
A DARK &
STORMY
NIGHT

SPOOKY

FOR A DARK &

COMPILED BY ALICE LOW ·

A BYRON PREISS BOOK · HYPERION

STORIES
STORMY NIGHT

ILLUSTRATED BY GAHAN WILSON

BOOKS FOR CHILDREN · NEW YORK

To Winston, Rosemary, Lila, and Xavier
with love and shivers
— A. L.

To trick-or-treaters everywhere
— G. W.

A Byron Preiss Book

Copyright © 1994 by Byron Preiss Visual Publications, Inc.
Illustrations © 1994 by Gahan Wilson and Byron Preiss Visual Publications, Inc.
All rights reserved. No part of this book may be used or reproduced in any manner whatsoever without written
permission from the publisher. Printed in the United States of America. For information, address
Hyperion Books for Children, 114 Fifth Avenue, New York, NY 10011.

FIRST EDITION

1 3 5 7 9 10 8 6 4 2

Library of Congress Cataloging-in-Publication Data
Spooky stories for a dark & stormy night/edited by Alice Low;
illustrated by Gahan Wilson—1st ed.
p. cm.
"A Byron Preiss book"—T.p. verso.
Summary: A collection of more than fifteen traditional and
original scary stories.
ISBN 0-7868-0012-7—ISBN 0-7868-2008-X (lib. bdg.)
1. Tales 2. Children's stories, American. 3. Children's
stories, English. [1. Folklore. 2. Horror stories. 3. Ghosts—
Fiction.] I. Low, Alice. II. Wilson, Gahan, ill.
PZ8.1.S283 1994
[398.2]—dc20 93-33638
CIP
AC
Stories selected by Alice Low
Book design by Leah Lococo/Louise Fili Ltd.
Executive Editor: Wendy Wax
Editorial Assistant: Vicky Rauhofer
Special thanks to Elizabeth Gordon, Andrea Cascardi, and Kristen Behrens

CONTENTS

INTRODUCTION

S O, YOU LIKE TO BE SCARED! JOIN THE CROWD! PEOPLE HAVE TOLD, LISTENED TO, OR WRITTEN SCARY STORIES ALL OVER THE WORLD FOR HUNDREDS OF YEARS. That shivery, quivery feeling we get when we read about old, deserted houses, wailing ghosts, mischievous goblins, and mean, powerful witches keeps us on the edge of our seats. And we enjoy hearing or reading gripping stories that make us want to *keep* reading. "What's going to happen next?" we ask ourselves as we hurry on to the next page.

The stories I have selected for this book will, I hope, make you ask that question. You will meet some fantastic characters—a monster named Dagger Claws, Washington Irving's Headless Horseman, Charles Dickens's evil Captain Murderer, and the dreaded witch of Russian folklore, Baba Yaga.

I chose the stories for this book with variety in mind. There are old tales, such as Isaac Bashevis Singer's "The Devil's Trick"; new stories, such as "Good-bye, Miss Patterson"; long stories, such as "The Legend of Sleepy Hollow"; and short stories like "Boo!" I also chose stories from different countries, such as "Bedtime Snacks" from southern China. Some stories are based on traditional folklore, handed down by word of mouth through generations, changing as the teller added his or her own touches, while keeping the main part of the tale intact.

Authors, too, have made their own changes in some of these old tales to heighten the scariness in spots, to make the story seem truer, or to make it even scarier.

Some of the stories have been written more recently than those based on folklore, such as "Duffy's Jacket," " 'My Neighbor Is a Monster, Pass It On,' " and "Uninvited Ghosts." Some stories included use repetition to build suspense or please the ear—"The Strange Visitor," for instance. And others end with a humorous twist—but I won't give those away by telling you here. And still others, such as "The Golden Arm," are scary down to the very last word.

I hope you will tell your own versions of these tales to your friends around a campfire, at a sleep over, or in a dark room. You might even want to go one step further and make up some spooky stories of your own.

—ALICE LOW

ON A WINDY, STORMY NIGHT...

TAILY-PO

AN AFRICAN AMERICAN FOLKTALE

RETOLD BY STEPHANIE CALMENSON

ONCE UPON A TIME, IN THE BIG DEEP WOODS, A MAN LIVED ALL BY HIMSELF. He had only one room and that room was his whole house: his sitting room, his bedroom, his dining room, and his kitchen, too.

One night, while the man was sitting at his fireplace stirring his stew for supper, the most curious creature you ever did see fell—*bonk!*—right down the chimney. It landed on its head. And its great, big tail landed right in the man's stew pot.

"Yeowwee!" screamed that thing. Well, that scared the man so that he grabbed his ax and started swinging it. While he was swinging—*whoops!*—he chopped the thing's tail off. The thing turned around and clawed its way right back up the chimney.

"That was a close call," said the man. He went back to stirring the stew—tail and all. In a little while, he sat down and ate. Then, with his stomach nice and full, the man went to bed and fell asleep in no time flat.

He hadn't been asleep very long when he was awakened by the sound of something *stomping, stomping, stomping* across the roof of his cabin. Whoever was up there was really mad. By and by, the man heard a voice say,

"Taily-po, taily-po;
Give me back my taily-po!"

Now the man would have been glad to give the tail back if he hadn't

eaten it. But try explaining that to a creature stomping across the roof of your house.

So the man called his dogs, Uno, Ino, and Cumptico-Calico. "Here! Here! Here!" he said. The dogs jumped up from where they were sleeping and chased that thing back into the big, deep woods.

"Good dogs!" said the man. Then he pulled the covers up and went back to sleep.

In the middle of the night, the man was awakened again. This time, he heard something *creeping, creeping, creeping* down the side of his cabin. By and by, he heard a voice say,

"Taily-po, taily-po;
Give me back my taily-po!"

The man sat straight up and looked out the window. Sure enough there were two great green upside-down eyes staring at him.

The man didn't wait one second before calling his dogs. "Here! Here! Here!" The dogs came bursting round the corner of the house. And they chased that thing away.

The man was shivering now from the sight of those great green upside-down eyes. This time he pulled the covers way up over his head before going back to sleep.

Just before daylight, the man was awakened one last time. Something was *scratching, scratching, scratching*—right at the foot of his bed!

The man peeked up over the covers. First he saw two little pointed ears. Then he saw two great green right-side-up eyes. He tried to call his dogs. "Here! Here! Here!" But he was so scared he had no voice.

The next thing the man knew, that thing pressed its nose right up to his and said,

"Taily-po, taily-po;
Give me back my taily-po!"

All at once the man got his voice back. "I haven't got your taily-po!" he said. And that thing said, "Yes you have."

Then the thing jumped on the man, turned him upside down, and shook, shook, shook him. And guess what? That tail fell right out, whole.

The man never saw that thing again. But if you visit him in the big, deep woods on a night when the moon shines bright and the wind blows cold, you'll hear a voice say,

"Taily-po, taily-po;
I got back my taily-po!"

CAPTAIN MURDERER

BY CHARLES DICKENS

RETOLD BY GEORGE HARLAND

WHEN I WAS A CHILD OF LESS THAN SIX YEARS OLD, LIVING IN CHATHAM, I HAD A NURSEMAID CALLED MARY WELLER. I always remember Mary for her bedtime stories, and one in particular sticks in my memory. Mary delighted in the macabre and horrific, and her bedtime stories were always tinged with this. The most horrific of the stories was kept for when I was ill, and being a sickly child, I heard it many, many times. Although I knew it word for word and could repeat it with her, I couldn't resist hearing it again and again.

"Now, Master Charles," she would say, "if you're a good little boy and take your lov'ly medicine, I'll tell you a nice little bedtime story."

I always fell for the ploy and would take my lov'ly medicine meekly, and tingled with excitement, my eyes closed, I would lie back on the pillows and wait.

"ONCE UPON A TIME, MASTER CHARLES, there was this gentleman called Captain Murderer."

Captain Murderer! He must have been an offshoot of the Bluebeard family, though I had no idea of that relationship in those days. His warning name appeared to have no effect on his neighbors, for he was admitted into the best society and possessed immense wealth. Captain

Murderer's mission in life was matrimony and the gratification of a cannibal appetite with tender young brides. . . .

On his marriage morning, dear, Captain Murderer had both sides of the way to church planted with curious flowers, and when the young bride saw them she would say, "Dear Captain Murderer, I never saw flowers like these before. What are they called?" and he would answer, "They are garnish for house—lamb!" and the way he laughed at his ferocious practical joke, displaying for the first time a row of very sharp teeth, had a disquieting effect on the minds of the noble bridal company, dear.

He always married in a coach and twelve, and all his noble horses were milk white except for one red spot on the back, which he caused to be hidden by the harness. For that spot *would* come there, though every horse was milk white when the Captain bought him. And that spot was young—bride's—blood, dear!

The wedding festivities went on for a whole month, and when all the guests had been dismissed and Captain Murderer was alone with his young bride, he would take out a golden rolling pin and a silver pie board. Now, there was this special feature about the Captain's courtship, dear. He would always ask if the young lady could make piecrust. If she couldn't, then she was taught.

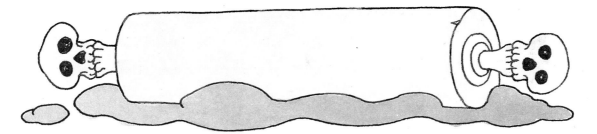

Well, when the young bride saw Captain Murderer produce the golden rolling pin and the silver pie board, she remembered this and turned up her laced silk sleeves to make a pie. The Captain brought out an enormous silver pie dish and flour and butter and eggs and all the things needed for the pie—except for the INSIDE.

The lovely young bride saw this, dear, and she said, "Dear Captain Murderer, what is this pie to be?"

"A meat pie!"

"But dear Captain Murderer, I see no meat."

"Look in the mirror!"

Well, dear, the young bride looked in the mirror, but of course still she saw no meat.

The Captain roared with laughter, and suddenly frowning, he drew out his sword and ordered her to roll out the crust.

So she rolled out the crust, dropping large tears upon it all the time because he was so cross. When she had lined the dish with the crust and had cut the crust to fit on the top, the Captain called out, "I see meat in the mirror!"

And the young bride looked up just in time to see the Captain cutting off her head, dear.

He chopped her into pieces, and peppered her, and salted her, and put her in the pie, and sent it to the baker's, and ate it all, and picked the bones, dear.

Captain Murderer went on in this way, prospering exceedingly, because the young brides all brought him handsome dowries—until he came to choose a bride from twin sisters. At first he didn't know which one to choose, for though one was fair and the other dark, they were both equally beautiful. But the fair twin loved him and the dark twin hated him, so naturally, he chose the fair one.

The dark twin would have prevented the marriage if she could, but she couldn't. However, on the night before it, she stole out and climbed his garden wall and looked in at his window through a chink in the shutter. She saw him having his teeth filed sharp by the family blacksmith. Next day she listened carefully and heard him make his joke about the house-lamb.

A month after the wedding day, dear, the fair twin rolled out the pastry, and Captain Murderer cut off her head, and chopped her into pieces, and peppered her, and salted her, and put her in the pie, and sent it to the baker's, and ate it all, and picked the bones, dear.

Now, the dark twin had had her suspicions much increased by the filing of the Captain's teeth and again by the house-lamb joke, so putting all things together when he gave out that her sister was dead, she guessed the truth and determined to have revenge. So she went up to the Captain's house and knocked on the knocker and pulled on the bell.

When Captain Murderer came to the door, she said, "Dear Captain Murderer, marry me next, for I always loved you and was jealous of my sister."

Well, dear, the Captain took this as a compliment and made a polite reply, and the marriage was soon arranged. Now, on the night before it, the dark twin again climbed to his window and again she saw him having his teeth filed sharp by the family blacksmith.

When she saw this she let out such a terrible laugh at the chink in the

shutter, that the Captain's blood curdled and he jumped up saying, "Oh, dear! I hope nothing I've eaten has disagreed with me!" At that she laughed again, a still more terrible laugh, and the Captain rushed to the window and opened the shutter, but she was nimbly gone and there was no one.

Next day they went to the church, dear, in a coach and twelve, and they were married. A month to the day later, as with all his other brides, the dark twin rolled out the pastry, and Captain Murderer cut off her head, and chopped her into pieces, and peppered her, and salted her, and put her in the pie, and sent it to the baker's, and ate it all, and picked the bones, dear.

But—before she had begun to roll out the pastry the dark twin had taken a deadly poison of the most awful character, distilled from toads' eyes and spiders' knees.

Captain Murderer had hardly picked her last bone when he began to swell, and to turn blue, and to be all over spots, and to scream. And he went on swelling, and turning bluer, and screaming louder than ever, until he stretched from floor to ceiling and wall to wall, and then, at one o'clock in the morning . . . he BLEW up with a loud explosion.

"Good night, Master Charles, and pleasant dreams."

WAIT TILL MARTIN COMES

AN AFRICAN AMERICAN FOLKTALE

RETOLD BY MARIA LEACH

THAT BIG HOUSE DOWN THE ROAD WAS HAUNT-
ED. NOBODY COULD LIVE IN IT. The door was never
locked. But nobody ever went in. Nobody would even spend
a night in it. Several people had tried but came running out pretty fast.

One night a man was going along that road on his way to the next village. He noticed that the sky was blackening. No moon. No stars.
Big storm coming for sure.

He had a long way to go. He knew he couldn't get home before it
poured.

So he decided to take shelter in that empty house by the road.

He had heard it was haunted. But shucks! Who believed in ghosts?
No such thing.

So he went in. He built himself a nice fire on the big hearth, pulled
up a chair, and sat down to read a book.

He could hear the rain beating on the windows. Lightning flashed.
The thunder cracked around the old building.

But he sat there reading.

Next time he looked up there was a little gray cat sitting on the hearth.

That was all right, he thought. Cozy.

He went on reading. The rain went on raining.

Pretty soon he heard the door creak and a big black cat came
sauntering in.

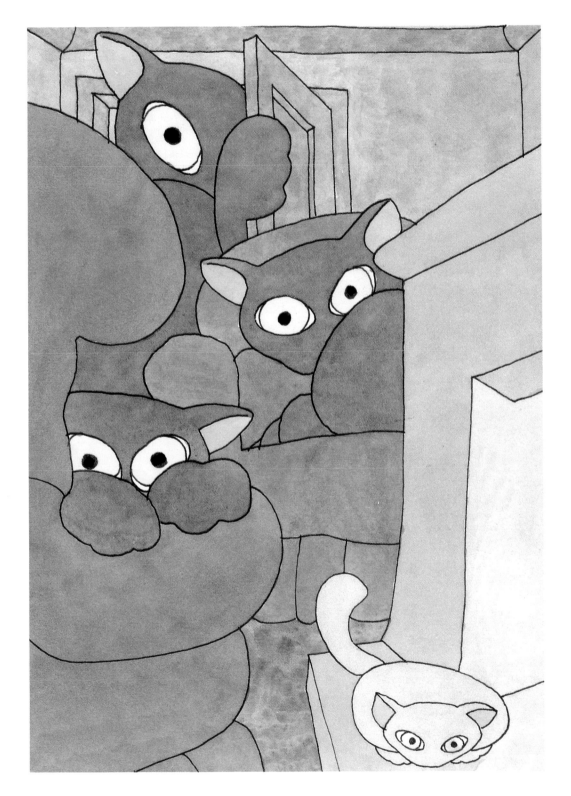

The first cat looked up.

"What we goin' to do with him?"

"Wait till Martin comes," said the other.

The man went right on reading.

Pretty soon he heard the door creak and another great big black cat, as big as a dog, came in.

"What we goin' to do with him?" said the first cat.

"Wait till Martin comes."

The man was awful scared by this time, but he kept looking in the book, pretending to be reading.

Pretty soon he heard the door creak and a great big black cat, as big as a calf, came in.

He stared at the man. "Shall we do it now?" he said.

"Wait till Martin comes," said the others.

The man just leaped out of that chair, and out the window, and down the road.

"Tell Martin I couldn't wait!" he said.

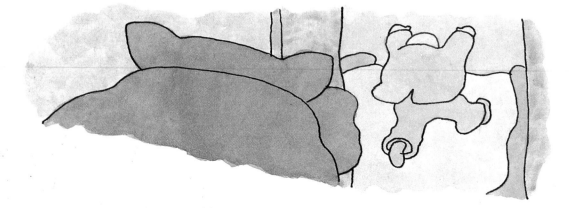

Down

a dark,

deserted

road...

THE LEGEND OF SLEEPY HOLLOW

BY WASHINGTON IRVING

RETOLD BY DELLA ROWLAND

NEAR THE BROAD EXPANSE OF THE HUDSON RIVER CALLED THE TAPPAN ZEE, THERE IS A SMALL VALLEY. Nestled among high hills, it is one of the quietest places in the whole world. This peaceful valley is such a drowsy, dreamy place that the Dutch farmers who settled it named it Sleepy Hollow.

Legend has it that Sleepy Hollow is bewitched. The people who live there often see strange lights or hear mysterious music and voices in the air. The sky has more shooting stars than anywhere else in the country, and the neighborhood is filled with "haunted" spots—at least, that's what the people say.

Over the years, farmfolk have passed down eerie tales of ghosts that have been seen in Sleepy Hollow. But there is one ghost story that is told more often than any other. It is the story of Ichabod Crane and the Headless Horseman.

IT ALL BEGAN DURING THE REVOLUTIONARY WAR when a soldier's head was blown off by a cannonball. His body was buried in the town churchyard. It was said that every evening his ghost rode back to the scene of the battle looking for his head. Many folks in the valley have claimed that when walking near the church just around midnight, they've felt a sudden blast of cold air. It was the Headless Horseman of Sleepy Hollow hurrying past, they'd say.

Some thirty years after the war, a schoolmaster named Ichabod Crane came to Sleepy Hollow. The name Crane certainly fit Ichabod, who looked exactly like one. He was tall and thin and had skinny, crooked bird legs and a pointed nose that looked like a beak. His hands dangled like broom ends from long, bony arms, and his big feet stuck out in front of him like wide, flat shovels. Walking down the road, one might have mistaken him for a scarecrow escaping from a cornfield.

Ichabod Crane was thin, but he had a huge appetite! He barely earned enough money from teaching school to satisfy his bottomless stomach. Luckily, he was able to live and eat with the families of the children he taught. Every week he lived with a different family, and to make himself useful, he helped with the chores and played with the children.

The families looked forward to Ichabod's visits. Moving from home to home, he became a sort of traveling newspaper for the farmers, carrying neighborhood news and gossip wherever he went. He could talk about any subject and make it interesting. But Ichabod was also popular with the local folks for another reason: He loved ghost stories.

Ghost stories were Ichabod's "most fearful pleasure." One of the few things he owned was a thick book of these stories. After his students had gone home each day, he would read from his book until it was too dark to see the words. The fearful part of this pleasure came when he had to walk home each evening through the shadowy swamps and woods. As he went along, every night sound reminded him of some awful event in a story he had just read. The moan of a whippoorwill

25

made him look over his shoulder. And the hoot of a screech owl startled him into running the rest of the way. Even the sudden flickering of fireflies filled him with terror.

When Ichabod was safely inside the house where he was staying, he would sit by the fire where no ghost would dare to enter. Then he happily spent the rest of the night telling stories from his book. The family, in turn, thrilled Ichabod with local tales of haunted places, goblins, and the Headless Horseman.

Another of Ichabod's pleasures was singing. Every Sunday, his quavery, nasal voice could be heard above everyone else's in the choir. And, once a week, he taught church hymns to the young people. His favorite pupil was Katrina Van Tassel.

Plump as a partridge and pink-cheeked as a peach, young Katrina was as beautiful as she was wealthy. Her father, Balthus Van Tassel, was the richest farmer in Sleepy Hollow. His huge house was full of mahogany furniture, old silver, and fine china; his barn was big as a church and bursting with grain from his fields. And his stables and barnyard were bustling with fine horses, fat pigs, milk cows, white geese, chickens, and ducks.

There wasn't a young man in the valley who didn't want to marry Katrina—including Ichabod. Twice a week, he'd come to the Van Tassel farm to give Katrina private singing lessons. Afterward, Katrina allowed him to stroll in the moonlit garden with her. She enjoyed Ichabod's company. He was more polite than many of the farmers, and he entertained her by quoting poetry and telling funny stories.

Katrina's attention gave Ichabod hope that she would marry him. But it was obvious that Katrina was also interested in Ichabod's rival, Brom Van Brunt. Nicknamed Brom Bones because of his size and strength, he was the hero of the valley. The farmfolk admired him because he was hardworking and good with horses, and they loved his mischievous sense of humor. Whenever any prank was played, people knew Brom Bones was surely the cause of it. Brom was always ready for a fight or some fun. He and his gang often galloped through the valley at night, whooping and hollering. Startled out of their sleep, the farmfolk would say, "There goes Brom Bones," and return to bed.

Brom wanted to fight Ichabod for Katrina. He boasted that he would "double the schoolmaster up and lay him on a shelf of his own school-house." But the puny schoolmaster was too smart to fight a battle he could never win. Since Ichabod wouldn't fight, Brom played practical jokes on him, hoping to make a fool of his ridiculous rival.

First Brom stopped up the school chimney, causing the school to fill up with smoke. As Ichabod's singing pupils came running out coughing, Brom sat on the roof and laughed. On other nights, he broke into the school and turned things topsy-turvy so that Ichabod thought ghosts were having meetings there. Worst of all, Brom gave Katrina a dog he had taught to imitate Ichabod's nasal singing voice. Whenever Ichabod began to sing, the dog would whine and drown out his voice.

But even though Brom's jokes made Ichabod look foolish, it seemed that the schoolmaster was Katrina's favorite.

One autumn afternoon, one of Balthus Van Tassel's messengers knocked on the school door. He handed Ichabod an invitation to attend a party at the Van Tassel farm that very evening. Ichabod was delighted. He had been planning to ask Katrina to marry him, and perhaps tonight would be the right time.

Ichabod dismissed school early and rushed back to Hans Van Ripper's farm, where he was lodging that week. Carefully he brushed his only suit and ran a comb through his scraggly hair.

Van Ripper offered Ichabod a horse so he could travel in style to see Katrina. But when Ichabod saw his steed, his heart sank. Gunpowder, once a fiery stallion, was now no more than a broken-down old plow horse that was blind in one eye. His backbone stuck up in a high scrawny ridge, and his tail and mane were knotted with burrs.

Ichabod was too polite to refuse his host's kind offer, so he climbed up on Gunpowder. But when he sat down in the saddle, the stirrups were so short that his knees were almost under his chin. This made his elbows stick out like a grasshopper's, and his arms flapped as Gunpowder slowly jogged along. But in spite of how he looked, Ichabod felt like a knight riding off to meet his princess.

When Ichabod arrived at the Van Tassel farm, Brom Bones was already the center of attention. All the guests were crowded around Brom in the yard, watching him keep Daredevil, his mischievous steed, under control. No one but Brom could handle this spirited horse.

Ichabod tied Gunpowder to a post in the barn. Then he joined the other guests as they went inside to eat. As Ichabod entered the parlor, he smiled with delight. Tables had been set up with all kinds of delicious Dutch dishes—autumn squash, corn; platters of ham, beef, chicken, and fish; cakes, pies, and preserves; apple cider and coffee.

Ichabod carefully tried each and every dish until his bottomless stomach felt pleasurably full. He couldn't wait for the day when he would be a member of this happy, well-fed household. He pictured Katrina's soft, beautiful face smiling up at him, the master of the household, as he enjoyed one of the many delicious meals they'd share.

Suddenly Ichabod heard music coming from the next room and hurried to find Katrina. He knew she loved to dance. Ichabod swung his lady love onto the dance floor, where he became a whirling dervish! Every bone and muscle wiggled and jiggled while he flapped his arms around and kicked up his heels. He made loving faces at Katrina, who smiled back politely. Children giggled and pointed at him until their mothers slapped their hands. Meanwhile, Brom Bones looked on jealously.

When the dancing ended, everyone retired to the porch to talk. Before long, their talk turned to ghost stories, and, of course, the favorite subject was the Headless Horseman.

One old farmer, who swore he didn't believe in ghosts, told about how he'd met the Headless Horseman one night near the churchyard. "He pulled me up behind him on his horse," the farmer said. "Then we galloped like the wind across the swamp. When we reached the bridge,

he turned into a skeleton before my very eyes, and threw me into the brook. I heard a thunderclap, and he jumped over the treetops and disappeared!"

Brom Bones spoke up next. "I ran into him, too, one night," he bragged. "I was on Daredevil so I said to the Horseman, 'I'll race you to the church bridge, and whoever wins has to buy the other a bowl of punch.' Daredevil beat him flat out, too, but when we came to the bridge, he bolted like a coward and vanished in a flash of fire."

Everyone laughed heartily at Brom's story. Ichabod laughed, too, but the thought of the Headless Horseman waiting in the woods somewhere made his blood run cold.

Other guests took turns at relating yarns about a haunted bridge or house, or a ghost chase. Ichabod told a few of the scariest tales from his book of ghost stories. Finally, the guests began to yawn and gathered their families together to head home.

Ichabod couldn't wait for the last wagon to rattle down the road. He knew that tonight was the perfect night to propose to Katrina.

As soon as they were alone, Ichabod boldly asked Katrina to marry him. His heart was pounding in his chest, and his hands shook as he waited for her answer. But he didn't have to wait long before she gave him the answer he dreaded. The poor schoolmaster was crushed when she said no. With a bent head, Ichabod left the house, walking straight to the barn without looking left or right. Quickly he mounted old Gunpowder, who was sleeping in a stall. After a few kicks, the horse stumbled through the gate.

By now it was the witching hour of midnight, a dismal time to be out in the woods alone. Suddenly all the ghosts and goblins that Ichabod had heard about that evening came creeping back into his thoughts. The night grew darker, and the stars seemed to sink deeper into the sky. Ichabod had never felt so lonely.

What was worse, he had come to a place where many of the ghost stories were supposed to have taken place. Up ahead, in the center of the road, stood an enormous tulip tree. Its huge gnarled limbs twisted down to the ground, then up again to the sky. Many townsfolk had seen strange visions near that tree.

When Ichabod approached the tree, he thought he saw something white hanging from one of its branches. But as he got closer, he saw it was only a spot where the tree's bark had been ripped off by lightning. Still, his teeth chattered and his knees knocked against the saddle as he passed by the tree.

A few yards from the tulip tree was a small stream that flowed into Wiley's Swamp. The bridge that crossed the stream was another well-known haunted spot. The closer Ichabod got to the bridge, the harder his heart thumped. Hoping to get across it quickly, he gave Gunpowder a few good kicks, but instead of hurrying, the horse froze and Ichabod almost went flying over his head.

At that moment, Ichabod heard something splash beside him in the stream. In the shadows of some trees he thought he saw a gigantic monster—part horse, part something else. He felt the hair on the back of his neck stand up. Summoning up his courage, he yelled out, "Wh-wh-who are you?" There was no answer.

Again Ichabod called out. Still there was no answer.

The silence was more than poor Ichabod could bear. Without realizing it, he began singing a hymn in a shaky voice. But his mouth was so dry that he could only croak out a few words. He kicked Gunpowder's sides as hard as he could, and finally the old horse clattered across the bridge.

Out of the corner of his eye, Ichabod saw that the monster was moving and that it was actually a horseman, wearing a black cloak, sitting on a huge black steed. Ichabod was seized with terror as he realized the silent figure was following him! When Gunpowder sped up, the mysterious rider also went faster. When Gunpowder slowed down, so did the shadowy creature. But no matter how fast or slow they moved, the dark horseman always stayed exactly the same distance away from Ichabod.

The two riders came out of the gloomy valley and onto a hill. In the moonlight, Ichabod was horror-struck to see that the traveler beside him had no head! "The Headless Horseman!" he gasped. Then he screeched. The horseman was carrying his pale head in his lap!

Desperately, Ichabod whipped Gunpowder, who took off like a bolt. But the dark horse reared up and followed right behind. Away they both dashed through the woods. Stones flew and sparks flashed whenever a hoof struck the ground. Ichabod stretched his long, thin body over Gunpowder's head, trying to make the horse move faster. The coattails of his jacket fluttered out behind him like a torn flag.

When they reached the road to Sleepy Hollow, Ichabod realized he was heading toward the church. He remembered the tales that had been told that evening. The Headless Horseman always disappeared at the churchyard bridge. "If I can make it to the bridge, I'll be safe," he told himself.

Just as he began to have hope, the saddle beneath him came loose and he began to slip off. Holding on tight to Gunpowder's neck, he managed to pull his feet out of the short stirrups just before the saddle fell off. As the saddle hit the ground, he heard it trampled underfoot by the demon rider behind him. Fear had made Ichabod's knees weak and it was all he could do to stay on Gunpowder as he bounced down the dark road.

Through a clearing in the trees, he could see the white walls of the church glaring in the moonlight. Luckily, the bridge was just ahead! The closer Ichabod got to the bridge, the closer the Headless Horseman came. The Headless Horseman had gained so much speed on Ichabod, that Ichabod could hear the black steed panting and feel its hot breath. Not daring to turn around, Ichabod kicked as hard as he could, and old Gunpowder sprang onto the bridge and thundered across.

Once he was on the other side of the bridge, Ichabod slowed down, sighing with relief. He turned to look behind him, expecting the Headless Horseman to have vanished just as he had in all those stories. But he hadn't! The ghostly Headless Horseman was still there!

Ichabod stared as the ghost stood up in his stirrups and hurled his awful head at him. Ichabod tried to dodge the gruesome missile but it hit his skull with a CRASH! and he tumbled down into the road.

THE NEXT MORNING, ICHABOD DID NOT COME TO breakfast, nor did he appear at the school that day. When he didn't appear for dinner as well, Hans Van Ripper organized a search party. Following the horse tracks from Van Tassel's, the farmers found the trampled saddle in the road. Next they found Gunpowder chomping

on grass in the churchyard. Near the bridge they saw Ichabod's hat lying next to a shattered pumpkin. But the schoolmaster was never found.

For days, people in Sleepy Hollow talked about the mysterious disappearance of Ichabod Crane. Finally, they decided that the Headless Horseman had carried him off.

Not long after that, Brom Bones married beautiful Katrina Van Tassel. Whenever the story of Ichabod Crane was told, Brom was always quiet until the pumpkin was mentioned. Then he would burst into a hearty laugh. This made some folks suspect that he knew more about the matter than he chose to tell. But then no one could really be sure.

Several years later, a farmer returned from New York swearing that he had seen Ichabod Crane in a crowd. But the folks who know the most about these matters were sure that Ichabod had been spirited away by the Headless Horseman.

Ichabod's schoolhouse was boarded up and was said to be haunted by the ghost of the schoolmaster. Even today, on a peaceful autumn evening, a farmer walking by it will usually hear a quavering nasal voice singing a church hymn.

THE DEVIL'S TRICK

A YIDDISH FOLKTALE

RETOLD BY ISAAC BASHEVIS SINGER

THE SNOW HAD BEEN FALLING FOR THREE DAYS AND THREE NIGHTS. Houses were snowed in and windowpanes covered with frost flowers. The wind whistled in the chimneys. Gusts of snow somersaulted in the cold air.

The devil's wife rode on her hoop, with a broom in one hand and a rope in the other. Before her ran a white goat with a black beard and twisted horns. Behind her strode the devil with his cobweb face, holes instead of eyes, hair to his shoulders, and legs as long as stilts.

In a one-room hut, with a low ceiling and soot-covered walls, sat David, a poor boy with a pale face and black eyes. He was alone with his baby brother on the first night of Hanukkah. His father had gone to the village to buy corn, but three days had passed and he had not returned home. David's mother had gone to look for her husband, and she too had not come back. The baby slept in his cradle. In the Hanukkah lamp flickered the first candle.

David was so worried he could not stay home any longer. He put on his padded coat and his cap with earflaps, made sure that the baby was covered, and went out to look for his parents.

That was what the devil had been waiting for. He immediately whipped up the storm. Black clouds covered the sky. David could hardly see in the thick darkness. The frost burned his face. The snow fell dry and heavy as salt. The wind caught David by his coattails and tried to lift him up off the ground. He was surrounded by laughter, as if from a thousand imps.

David realized the goblins were after him. He tried to turn back and go home, but he could not find his way. The snow and darkness swallowed everything. It became clear to him that the devils must have caught his parents. Would they get him also? But heaven and earth have vowed that the devil may never succeed completely in his tricks. No matter how shrewd the devil is, he will always make a mistake, especially on Hanukkah.

The powers of evil had managed to hide the stars, but they could not extinguish the single Hanukkah candle. David saw its light and ran toward it. The devil ran after him. The devil's wife followed on her hoop, yelling and waving her broom, trying to lasso him with her rope. David ran even more quickly than they, and reached the hut just ahead of the devil. As David opened the door the devil tried to get in with him. David managed to slam the door behind him. In the rush the devil's tail got stuck in the door.

"Give me back my tail," the devil screamed.

And David replied, "Give me back my father and mother."

The devil swore that he knew nothing about them, but David did not let himself be fooled.

"You kidnapped them, cursed Devil," David said. He picked up a sharp ax and told the devil that he would cut off his tail.

"Have pity on me. I have only one tail," the devil cried. And to his wife he said, "Go quickly to the cave behind the black mountains and bring back the man and woman we led astray."

His wife sped away on her hoop and soon brought the couple back. David's father sat on the hoop holding on to the witch by her hair; his mother came riding on the white goat, its black beard clasped tightly in her hands.

"Your mother and father are here. Give me my tail," said the devil.

David looked through the keyhole and saw his parents were really there. He wanted to open the door at once and let them in, but he was not ready to free the devil.

He rushed over to the window, took the Hanukkah candle, and singed the devil's tail. "Now, Devil, you will always remember," he cried, "Hanukkah is no time for making trouble."

Then at last he opened the door. The devil licked his singed tail and ran off with his wife to the land where no people walk, no cattle tread, where the sky is copper and the earth is iron.

A NORWEGIAN FOLKTALE

RETOLD BY MARGARET READ MACDONALD

ONCE THERE WAS A LITTLE BOY WHO WAS SO PLUMP AND FAT THAT HIS MOTHER CALLED HIM LITTLE BUTTERCUP. One day when his mother was kneading bread the DOG began to bark!

"Run quick, Little Buttercup, and see why Goldtooth the Dog is barking," said his mother.

So Buttercup ran out.

"Oh Mother, Mother . . . it's the Troll Hag coming over the hill with her head under her arm and a bag on her back!"

"Quick, Little Buttercup . . . hide beneath my breadboard. And when she comes in . . . don't make a peep."

So Little Buttercup hid under his mother's breadboard.

IN came the TROLL HAG.

"Good day," said the Troll Hag. "Where's Little Buttercup today?"

"Oh, he's out with his father . . . hunting pigeons," said Buttercup's mother.

"What a pity. I have a little silver knife as a present for Little Buttercup. It's a pity he's not here."

When Little Buttercup heard that he could not contain himself.

"Oh Pip, Pip . . . here I am!" he called. And out he came from under the breadboard. "Here I am! Where's my little silver knife?"

"It's right here in my bag," said the Troll Hag. "Just crawl inside and fetch it out."

So that foolish Little Buttercup crawled into the witch's bag to get his little silver knife.

As soon as he was in the bag the Troll Hag threw the bag over her shoulder and tromped off over the hill chanting,

Buttercup Soup
Buttercup Soup
Buttercup Soup
Buttercup Soup

After a while she became tired and sat down under a tree to rest. "Tell me, Little Buttercup . . . how far is it off to Snoring?" (This Troll Hag lived at Snoring.)

"Oh, it's a long way to Snoring," said Little Buttercup. "I think five or six miles."

"Then I'd better have a nap," said the Troll Hag. And she lay down and fell asleep.

While she slept, Buttercup took his little silver knife, cut a hole in the bag, and crept out. Then Buttercup found a heavy fir tree root and put

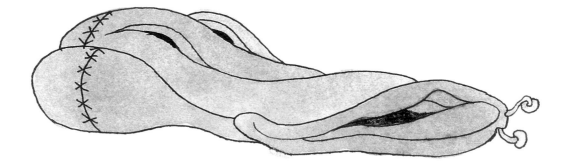

the root in the bag in his place. Then Buttercup ran away home to his mother.

When the Troll Hag reached home she dumped out her bag and found only a fir tree root!

Next day Buttercup's mother was kneading her bread when the DOG began to bark!

"Run quick, Little Buttercup, and see why Goldtooth the Dog is barking."

Little Buttercup ran out.

"Oh Mother, Mother . . . it's the Troll Hag coming over the hill with her head under her arm and a bag on her back."

"Quick, Little Buttercup . . . hide beneath my breadboard. And when she comes in . . . don't make a peep."

So Little Buttercup hid under his mother's breadboard.

IN came the TROLL HAG.

"Good day," said the Troll Hag. "Where's Little Buttercup today?"

"Oh, he's out with his father . . . hunting wild ducks."

"What a pity. I have a little silver fork in my bag as a present for Little Buttercup. It's a pity he's not here."

When Little Buttercup heard this he could not contain himself.

"Oh Pip, Pip . . . here I am!" he called. And out he came from under the breadboard. "Here I am! Where's my little silver fork?"

"It's right here in my bag," said the Troll Hag. "Just crawl inside and fetch it out."

So that foolish Little Buttercup crawled into the witch's bag to get his little silver fork. As soon as he was in the bag the Troll Hag threw the bag over her shoulder and tromped off over the hill chanting,

Buttercup Soup
Buttercup Soup
Buttercup Soup
Buttercup Soup

After a while she began to feel tired and sat down under a tree to rest.

"Tell me, Little Buttercup . . . how far is it off to Snoring?"

"Ohhhh, it's a long way to Snoring," said Little Buttercup. "I think ten or eleven miles."

"Then I'd better have a nap," said the Troll Hag. And she lay down and fell asleep.

While she slept, Buttercup took his little silver fork and poked a hole through the bag. Buttercup found a large stone. He put the stone in the bag in his place. Then Little Buttercup ran away home to his mother.

When the Troll Hag reached home she dumped out her bag and found a great heavy stone!

Next morning Buttercup's mother was kneading her bread when the DOG began to bark!

"Run quick, Little Buttercup, and see why Goldtooth the Dog is barking," said his mother.

So Buttercup ran out.

"Oh Mother, Mother . . . it's the Troll Hag coming over the hill with her head under her arm and a bag on her back!"

"Quick, Little Buttercup . . . hide beneath my breadboard. And when she comes in . . . don't make a peep."

So Little Buttercup hid under his mother's breadboard.

IN came the TROLL HAG.

"Good day," said the Troll Hag. "Where's Little Buttercup today?"

"Oh, he's out with his father . . . hunting ptarmigan."

"What a pity. I had a little silver spoon as a present for Little Buttercup. It's a pity he's not here."

When Little Buttercup heard that . . . that foolish boy could not contain himself.

"Oh Pip, Pip . . . here I am!" he called. And out he came from under the breadboard. "Here I am! Where's my little silver spoon?"

"It's right here in my bag," said the Troll Hag. "Just crawl inside and fetch it out."

So Little Buttercup crawled into the Troll Hag's bag to get his little silver spoon.

As soon as Buttercup was in the bag the Troll Hag threw the bag over her shoulder and tromped off over the hill chanting,

> Buttercup Soup
> Buttercup Soup
> Buttercup Soup
> Buttercup Soup

After a while she became tired and sat down under a tree to rest.

"Tell me, Little Buttercup . . . how far is it off to Snoring?"

"Ohhhh, it's a long way to Snoring," said Little Buttercup, "I think fifteen or twenty miles."

"Then I'd better have a nap," said the Troll Hag.

And she started to lie down. . . .

"Twenty miles! But that's impossible!" said the witch. "You have cheated me twice, Little Buttercup. But not THIS time." And she threw the bag over her back once more and tromped off over the hills chanting,

Buttercup Soup
Buttercup Soup
Buttercup Soup
Buttercup Soup

When the Troll Hag reached her home she called her Troll Daughter.

"Here's Little Buttercup come for dinner. You must chop off his head and stew him in the pot while I go invite the guests."

When the Troll Hag was gone the Troll Daughter took Buttercup to the chopping block. But how to chop off his head? She did not know. She held the ax this way . . . and that way. . . . Still she seemed not to know how to chop.

"Would you like me to show you how?" said Little Buttercup. "It's really quite simple. Just put your head right here and hand me the ax."

So Little Buttercup chopped off the head of the Troll Daughter and put her into the stew pot. Then Little Buttercup climbed up onto the chimney and waited for the Troll Hag to come home. He carried up with him the fir root and the large stone. When the Troll Hag came home she went straight to her stew pot and tasted the broth.

"Mmmm, mmmm . . .
Good by my troth
Buttercup BROTH!"

But Little Buttercup called down the chimney,

"Good by my troth

TROLL broth!"

Then the Troll Hag tasted the soup again.

"Mmmm, mmmm . . .

Good by my troth

Buttercup BROTH!"

But Little Buttercup called down the chimney,

"Good by my troth

TROLL broth!"

A third time the Troll Hag tasted the soup.

"Mmmm, mmmm . . .

Good by my troth

Buttercup BROTH!"

Then she looked up the chimney to see if the echo would come again.

So Little Buttercup threw the stone and the fir root right down the chimney, calling,

"Good by my troth

TROLL broth!"

And the heavy stone and the fir root knocked that Troll Hag right into the pot herself.

Little Buttercup called out,

"Good by my troth

It's DOUBLE troll broth!"

Then he took his little silver knife and his little silver fork and his little silver spoon and went along home to his mother.

WILEY AND THE HAIRY MAN

AN AFRICAN AMERICAN FOLKTALE

RETOLD BY DELLA ROWLAND

WILEY AND HIS MAMA AND DADDY LIVED NEAR THE SWAMPS OF THE TOMBIGBEE RIVER. One day Wiley's daddy went out on the river in his rowboat to catch some catfish, and that night Wiley found his daddy's empty rowboat bumping against the sandy riverbank. "He fell in," everybody said, and they searched for him in the Tombigbee River and along the riverbanks. Then they heard a big ugly laugh coming from the swamps. "It's the Hairy Man," they all said, and they stopped looking. They knew the Hairy Man had put Wiley's daddy in his sack.

Back home, Wiley's mama told him, "Wiley, now that the Hairy Man's got your papa, he won't be happy till he gets you, too. You make sure you take your hound dogs with you when you go wandering in the swamp. The Hairy Man can't stand to be near a dog." Wiley listened to his mama because she knew swamp magic as good as the Hairy Man did.

Not long after that Wiley had to go into the swamp to chop some poles so he could build a chicken house. He made sure he took his hound dogs with him so the Hairy Man couldn't get him. When he was about a mile into the swamp, a wild pig ran right in front of those hounds. They took off after it, leaving Wiley all by himself in the gloomy swamp. "I sure hope the Hairy Man isn't around here," he thought.

Holding his ax real tight, Wiley looked to the right of him. No Hairy Man. He looked to the left. Still no Hairy Man. He turned and looked behind him. No Hairy Man there either. But when he turned back around, there was the Hairy Man not more than three feet in front of him. He sure was ugly. He was hairy all over. His eyes were red and glowing like a fire. His teeth were big and white and sharp. The Hairy Man opened up his sack and grinned at Wiley.

Wiley looked down at the sack and caught a glimpse of the Hairy Man's feet below it—they were cow's feet! Since he'd never seen a cow that could climb a tree, he decided that's just what he would do. He hightailed it up a tall bay tree.

"Why'd you climb that tree?" the Hairy Man called up.

"My mama told me to stay away from you," Wiley said. "What you got in your sack?"

"Nothing yet," grinned the Hairy Man. Then he picked up Wiley's ax and began chopping down the tree. The ax started swinging and the wood chips started flying.

Now Wiley had learned a little swamp magic from his mama, so he rubbed his stomach against the bay tree and hollered out, "Fly, chips, fly! Back to your same place!"

At that, the chips flew back to the tree trunk where the Hairy Man had just chopped. This made the Hairy Man mad and he started chopping all the faster. The faster he chopped, the louder Wiley hollered, till the chips were flying back and forth so fast they didn't know which way was up or down or sideways. Wiley hollered till he was hoarse but he could see that the Hairy Man was gaining on him.

Wiley had just about hollered himself out when he heard his hound dogs yelping. "HEEEERE, dogs!" Wiley hollered, with the very last of his voice.

"Stop hollering for those dogs!" cried the Hairy Man. "I sent a pig for them to chase." But the dogs had caught a whiff of the Hairy Man and were running toward him fast as lightning.

"AAAHHHHHHHH!" The Hairy Man tore through the trees and raced back to the swamp hollering so loud that Wiley's mama could hear him from her kitchen, where she was making Wiley's dinner.

When Wiley got home, he told his mama about the Hairy Man almost putting him in the sack.

"The Hairy Man is after you, for sure," Wiley's mama said. "Next time you see him, don't climb up a tree. Just stay on the ground and say, 'Hello, Hairy Man.'" Then Wiley's mama told him exactly what else to say to the Hairy Man. The last thing she said was, "And this time, leave the hound dogs at home."

Wiley didn't want to go anywhere without the hound dogs, but he knew better than to go against his mama. His mama knew swamp magic as good as the Hairy Man did.

The next day, Wiley tied up his dogs so they couldn't follow him and walked into the swamp alone. He didn't have to go far before he looked up and there was the Hairy Man with his sack slung over his shoulder.

"Hello, Hairy Man," Wiley said.

The Hairy Man just grinned and took his sack off his shoulder. Wiley had to will his feet to stay put on the ground and not climb a tree. Then he did what his mama told him.

"I hear you're the best magic man around here," he said.

"I reckon I am," said the Hairy Man, and he moved closer.

"I bet you can't turn yourself into a giraffe," said Wiley, trying not to step back.

"I can but I don't feel like it," grinned the Hairy Man, and he opened up his sack.

"I know you can't do it," said Wiley.

"Can so," said the Hairy Man, and he twisted around until he turned himself into a giraffe with big sharp teeth. The giraffe swung its long neck around Wiley's shoulders and grinned in his face.

Wiley was shaking in his shirt, for it was too late to climb a bay tree, but he said, "I . . . I . . . I bet you can't turn yourself into an alligator."

The giraffe twisted and turned itself into an alligator with long snapping jaws. Each time those jaws snapped shut they grinned at Wiley.

"Anybody can turn himself into something big," said Wiley. "I bet you can't turn yourself into something small, like a possum."

The alligator twisted around and turned into a possum. As soon as it did, Wiley grabbed it and stuffed it into the sack. He tied the top real tight and threw the sack into the Tombigbee River. Then he started for home with a grin on his face as big as the Hairy Man's to tell his mama that her plan had worked.

Wiley hadn't walked five steps and there was the Hairy Man. "I turned myself into the wind and blew out of the sack," the Hairy Man said.

Zip! Wiley was up a bay tree before the Hairy Man had even finished his sentence. He sat there all afternoon thinking about the Hairy Man waiting on the ground and about his hound dogs tied up at home.

Finally, Wiley hollered down, "Hairy Man, I bet you can't make things disappear."

"That's what I'm best at," bragged the Hairy Man. "Look at your shirt."

Wiley looked down and saw there wasn't even a button left. "That was easy," he said. "What about this rope belt I got tied around my pants?"

"Hah!" the Hairy Man snorted. "I can make all the rope in the county disappear!"

As soon as Wiley saw his rope belt disappear, he knew the ropes holding his dogs were gone, too, so he threw his head back and hollered, "HEEEERE, dogs! HEEEERE, dogs!" And the Hairy Man ran off into the swamp again.

When Wiley got home, he told his mama about the Hairy Man turning into the wind and blowing himself out of the sack and about making the ropes disappear.

"Don't worry, son," his mama told him. "You've fooled the Hairy Man twice now. If you fool him three times, he'll have to leave you alone. I've got a plan. Go get a baby pig and put it in your bed. Then light a fire in the fireplace and climb up in the loft. Stay there no matter what happens."

Wiley did what his mama told him because she knew swamp magic as good as the Hairy Man did. He hadn't been in the loft long when he heard the wind howling and the trees shaking and the dogs barking. He peeked through a hole in the wall and saw the dogs pulling at their ropes and looking toward the swamp. The hair on their back was standing up, and their lips were pulled back in a snarl.

Suddenly from out of the swamp ran an animal, the likes of which Wiley had never seen before. It was as big as a mule and had horns on

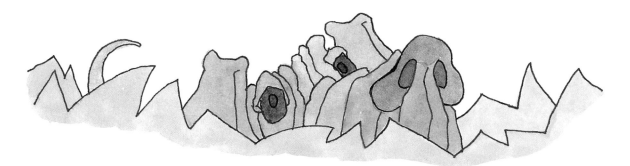

its head. One of the dogs jerked and jumped so hard it broke its rope and ran off after the beast. Then an even bigger animal with a long pointed nose and glowing teeth ran out of the swamp and growled at the cabin. Wiley's other dog broke loose and took off after it. Wiley knew the Hairy Man had sent those animals to get rid of the hounds. And he knew that soon the Hairy Man would be coming.

Sure enough, Wiley heard something like cow's feet scrambling around on the roof just above him. The Hairy Man was trying to get into the house through the fireplace. But when he touched the hot chimney, he howled and ranted so, that Wiley was ashamed for his mama to hear such things. Then Wiley heard the Hairy Man climb down off the roof and knock on the front door just as bold as you please!

"Mama!" the Hairy Man hollered, "I've come for your baby."

"You can't have him," Mama hollered right back.

"Give him to me or I'll set your house on fire," the Hairy Man shouted.

"I'll put it out with milk," sang Mama in a voice as sweet as syrup.

"I'll dry up your water, make your cow go dry, and send a million boll weevils out of the ground to eat up your cotton!" the Hairy Man said.

"You wouldn't be so mean, would you?" Mama said.

"I'm the meanest man I know," answered the Hairy Man.

"If I give you my baby, will you go away and leave everything else alone?" Mama asked.

"That's just what I'll do!" grinned the Hairy Man.

Wiley heard his mama open up the door. He was shaking so hard, he could hardly crawl over to a hole in the floor so he could see what was going to happen next.

"He's over there," Mama said, pointing to Wiley's bed.

The Hairy Man grinned bigger than he ever had in the swamp. He clomped over to the bed and snatched back the covers. "Hey!" he hollered. "This is a baby pig!"

"I didn't say what kind of baby I was giving you," Mama told him, "and that baby pig was mine before I gave it to you. So there."

By now the Hairy Man was so mad he stomped all over the house, hissing and yelling, and shaking his hairy arms and head, and grinding his big teeth. But he'd been fooled three times, and his magic was no good on Wiley and his mama. Finally, he ran out the door and tore through the swamp. He was so mad he left a path ten feet wide where he had pulled up the trees by their roots.

After a while, the swamp grew back and covered up the path the Hairy Man had made. But Wiley always made sure he took his hound dogs with him whenever he went into the swamp.

STANDS

A STRANGE

AND CREEPY

HOUSE . . .

"MY NEIGHBOR IS A MONSTER, PASS IT ON"

BY ERIC WEINER

ON MONDAY MORNING, MELANIE GOLD WATCHED FROM HER BEDROOM WINDOW AS A BLACK MOVING VAN DROVE SLOWLY PAST HER HOUSE. It was her new neighbor, Mr. Bartok. He was moving into the little brown house at the end of Melanie's dead-end street.

That afternoon, while playing in the backyard with some neighborhood friends, Melanie whispered in Billy Walsh's ear, "Our new neighbor is a monster. Pass it on."

Billy smirked and did as he was told. He passed it on, whispering the rumor to his older sister Ruthie. "Pass it on," Billy told Ruthie. And she did. That night at dinner, she passed the rumor on to her best friend Chloe. Who passed the rumor on to her cousin Steven. Who passed it on . . .

And on and on and on the rumor went. So that by recess at school the next day, kids were coming up to Melanie and telling her her own rumor back again!

Of course, the rumor had changed some by then. Now kids were saying that at night Mr. Bartok flew around his house like a giant wild bee. That when the sun went down, his hands turned into sharp claws. That in the darkness Melanie's new neighbor sprouted fangs and grew fur on his head like a vampire bat.

Bradleyville was a small town. Kids talked to their parents, parents talked to other parents—and the rumor about Melanie's neighbor spread and spread until it seemed like the whole town was buzzing about Mr. Bartok. One kid who lived right next door to Mr. Bartok told Melanie that she had heard loud monster screeches coming from Mr. Bartok's house late at night. Another kid who lived far away from Mr. Bartok told Melanie that he had seen him flying past his window at three in the morning.

And as Melanie heard her own rumor over and over, a strange thing happened. She started to believe it.

After all, Mr. Bartok did look kind of weird, with that shiny bald head and those thick black-framed glasses. "Who knows," she thought. "Maybe Mr. Bartok does turn into a monster at night!"

With each passing day, Melanie grew more and more curious. Until one night, she couldn't stand it any longer. She had to know if the rumor was true.

Melanie knew that her mother would never give her permission to visit Mr. Bartok. So she didn't ask. She just waited until her parents went to bed, then crept downstairs, threw on her mother's black cape, and slipped out into the cold, dark night.

It began raining almost at once. Thunder boomed and lightning cracked. Dark sheets of rain beat down against the streets of Bradleyville.

Despite the cape, Melanie was sopping by the time she reached Mr. Bartok's house at the end of the street. The storm had knocked out the streetlights. But just then a streak of lightning zigzagged down and lit up everything. And Melanie saw that the shades on the windows of Mr.

Bartok's house were all pulled down. Melanie shivered at the sight. She felt a very strong desire to turn and run.

"No," she told herself. "I have to do this. I have to see Mr. Bartok."

And she forced herself up the narrow walk.

The front door was ajar. She went in and stood trembling in the dark foyer. "Mr. Bartok?"

There was no answer.

Melanie's heart was pounding. "This is silly," she told herself. How could she get so scared about her own rumor?

A rounded archway led to another room. Melanie walked slowly through . . .

"Mr. Bartok?"

BANG!!!

The noise was so loud and sudden that Melanie screamed. Then she realized what the noise was. Just another thunderclap, outside the house.

Melanie almost fainted with relief. In fact, she felt so relieved that she started to laugh. Once she started laughing, she couldn't stop. She laughed louder and louder. Imagine believing a rumor she had started herself! Ha-ha-ha! How stupid, how foolish, how silly, how—

Something moved in the next room.

Melanie stopped laughing with a gasp. Her heart started racing.

And then Mr. Bartok the monster flew into the room. . . .

BEDTIME SNACKS

A CHINESE AMERICAN FOLKTALE

BY LAURENCE YEP

WHEN SHAKEY HEARD THE THUMP ON THE ROOF, HE JERKED HIS HEAD UP TO STARE AT THE CEILING. "WHAT WAS THAT?".

His greedy little brother had already picked out the biggest bowl of rice. "It's just some old cat. Why are you such a coward?"

Shakey had gotten his nickname because every strange noise and shadow frightened him. Even so, he didn't see it that way. "I'm not a coward. I'm just cautious."

"That's good," their mother said, "but you go too far sometimes." She opened the door. "I'm going to visit some friends, so your Auntie will come to baby-sit."

Shakey put a finger to his lips. "Shh, Momma. You never know who might be listening."

"I think you're safe enough dear; but even so, don't open to anyone but Auntie." Mother closed the door.

Up on the roof, the monster, Dagger Claws, merely smiled and waited.

Meanwhile, as Shakey lowered the crossbar across the door inside the house, his little brother mocked him. "Scaredy-cat, scaredy-cat."

Shakey sat down next to his little brother. "If you listened to your head more than your belly, you'd be scared, too."

The two brothers had finished their meals and were washing the dishes when their elderly Auntie came to the door. Instantly Dagger Claws

leaped down and killed the poor old woman with one swipe of her big claws.

When he heard the thud outside, Shakey was so scared that he dropped a rice bowl. It cracked on the floor, but he ignored the pieces. "Who's . . . who's there?" he called.

"Just your Auntie," Dagger Claws said in a high voice.

Crunch, crunch, crunch. Her big jaws munched on poor Auntie's bones.

Although he had already finished his dinner, the little brother was still hungry. One bowl of rice and a few vegetables were not enough for him. "Are you eating something good, Auntie?"

"Chestnuts," Dagger Claws lied. "Luscious, crisp chestnuts."

"Let me have some." The little brother ran to the door and lifted the bar.

Dagger Claws gobbled down the rest of poor old Auntie. "Only if you go to bed right now and put out the candle."

Shakey threw himself at the door before his little brother could open it. He was so scared that his teeth were chattering. "Wh-wh-why?"

"It hurts your poor old Auntie's eyes." Dagger Claws hurriedly put on Auntie's dress. She wanted two tasty little boys for her dessert.

The younger boy ran over to the big red candle to blow it out. Shakey darted after him and grabbed hold of his eager little brother. "But I don't like the dark, Auntie."

Dagger Claws scratched at the door. Her sharp claws left grooves in the wood. "Shame on you! You're a big boy now. Well, if you won't be nice to me, I won't be nice to you. No bedtime snacks."

"No, don't do that," the little brother said, and blew out the candle before Shakey could stop him.

The instant she saw the light go out underneath the door, Dagger Claws kicked it open with a bang. Shakey was so startled that he let go of his little brother.

For a moment, the moonlight silhouetted Dagger Claws. They saw nothing wrong because she looked like a round woman in a dress. Then she stepped in and shut the door so it was black inside the house. "Now get in bed, boys."

Shakey tried to get hold of his little brother, but he was already groping his way through the dark over to his sleeping mat.

"I'm over here, Auntie," the little brother called.

Dagger Claws stumbled blindly through the house. "Where?"

"Here, Auntie. Right here," the little brother said eagerly.

Dagger Claws followed the voice right to the sleeping mats. The next moment she had begun her own little snack. *Crunch, crunch, crunch.*

Shakey listened to Dagger Claws smack her lips and munch away happily. Shivering, he asked, "Little brother?"

Shakey was so frightened that he could not move. "Is that you, little brother?" Shakey asked.

"He's busy eating his chestnuts," Dagger Claws said.

Crunch, crunch, crunch.

When Dagger Claws was almost finished, she called to Shakey. "Where are you? There's plenty of crisp, luscious chestnuts for everyone."

But Shakey was still so scared that he hunted for an excuse to stay where he was. "Aren't you thirsty?"

Both Auntie and the little brother had been rather salty, so Dagger Claws said, "I am a little thirsty."

"I'll get you a drink, Auntie," he offered.

Dagger Claws settled back. "What a sweet little boy." After a drink of water, she would have her third and last course.

Shakey forced himself to be calm. Hardly daring to breathe, he took a step. Then he took another and almost slipped on the wet floor. He tried not to think about why the floor was wet. He took a third step. The crunching began again. He looked neither to the right nor to the left. Instead, he kept his eyes right on the door.

When he was outside, Shakey lowered the bucket into the well. Then he backed away. "Auntie, the bucket is too heavy. Come and help me."

"Just a moment. The moonlight hurts my eyes, too." Dagger Claws rummaged around blindly until she found a basket. She dumped out the rice that was inside and put it over her head. Then she hid her big paws inside the sleeves of the dress. When she stepped outside the house, she could still see through the sides of the basket.

Shakey could not see her fangs or her paws, but he could see the strange tail that stuck out from under the dress. It whipped around in excitement. Then he knew Auntie was really a monster. It was too late to save Auntie or his little brother. He would be lucky to save himself.

It was a funny thing, but now that Shakey's worst fears were real, he wasn't scared anymore. Waiting had been the hardest part.

"There, Auntie." He pointed at the well.

Dagger Claws bent over the well. With her paws still inside her sleeves, she began to pull at the bucket's rope. "A strong boy like you can't lift a little bucket like this?"

Shakey ran to the well and shoved Dagger Claws with all his strength. With a screech, the monster fell headfirst down the well.

She landed with a big splash. Water rose up the well and crashed around the sides.

"I'll fix you!" she shrieked. She sank her long, hard claws into the sides of the well. *Thunk, thunk.* She pulled herself out of the water. "I'll start with your toes first so you can watch me eat you." Slowly she began to climb up the sides. "You can run. You can hide. But I'll find you."

Shakey knew he didn't have much time. He picked up a long bamboo pole that lay next to the well and tied a big block of stone to the pole.

Dagger Claws was almost out of the well when Shakey lifted the long, heavy pole and swung the free end.

Dagger Claws dodged but some of the blows struck her. That only made her even angrier. "Just for that, I'm going to take you to my cave," she growled. "And I'm going to eat you slowly. One piece a day."

But Shakey kept poking and swinging at her until Dagger Claws lifted one paw and caught the bamboo pole. Her claws sank deep into the wood. "Hah! I've got your little stick now."

As she yanked at the pole, Shakey let go so that the pole went into the well and the stone followed the pole. Dagger Claws stared at the stone that fell past her.

Then the stone was pulling the pole after it. Too late, Dagger Claws tried to let go of the pole, but her sharp claws were embedded in its sides. Still holding the pole, Dagger Claws was yanked from the wall of the well.

Stone, pole, and monster splashed into the water, but this time Dagger Claws followed the stone down through the water. Down, down, down to the bottom of the well where she drowned.

They buried Shakey's little brother and Auntie and capped the well. And after that, when Shakey's mother visited friends, Shakey always went along with her.

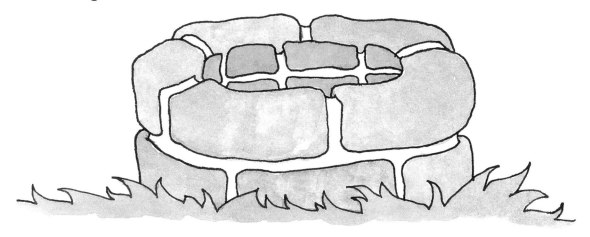

THE BLACK GEESE

A   R U S S I A N   F O L K T A L E

R E T O L D   B Y   A L I S O N   L U R I E

LONG AGO THERE LIVED A MAN AND WIFE WHO HAD TWO CHILDREN, A GIRL AND A BOY. One day the woman said to her daughter, "Elena, we are going to market today; stay in the house while we are away, and look after your baby brother, for Baba Yaga's black geese who steal children have been seen flying over the village. When we come home, we will bring you some sugar buns."

After her mother and father were gone, Elena stayed in the house with her brother for a little while. But soon she got tired of this and took him outside to where her friends were playing. She put him down on the grass and joined in their games, and presently she forgot all about him and ran off. The black geese came down, seized the little boy, and carried him away.

When Elena came back and found her brother gone, she was very frightened. She rushed to look in every corner of the house and yard, but could not see him. She shouted his name, but he did not answer. At last she said to herself that the black geese must have stolen her brother and taken him to Baba Yaga, the terrible witch of the forest, who is eight feet tall and eats little children. "I must go after him," Elena said. And she began to run toward the forest.

She ran across the fields and came to a pond, and there she saw a fish lying on the bank, gasping for water.

"Elena, Elena!" it called. "I am dying!"

Elena wanted to hurry on, but she was sorry for the fish. So she picked it up and put it carefully in the pond, where it sank and then rose again to the surface. "As you have helped me, so I shall help you," said the fish. "Here, take this shell. If ever you are in danger, throw it over your shoulder."

Elena did not see how a shell could help her, but she did not want to seem rude, so she put it in her pocket and ran on. Presently she came to a grove of trees, and there she saw a squirrel caught in a trap.

"Elena, Elena!" it called. "My leg is caught!" Elena wanted to go on, but she felt sorry for the squirrel. So she released the trap. The squirrel darted up into a tree and down again. "As you have helped me, so I shall help you," it said. "Here, take this walnut. If ever you are in danger, throw it over your shoulder."

Elena put the nut in her pocket and hurried on. Soon she came to a stony bank, and there she saw a field mouse trying to move a fallen rock.

"Elena, Elena!" it called. "I cannot get into my hole!" Elena was sorry for the field mouse, so she pushed and shoved until she had moved the rock aside. The mouse darted into its hole and reappeared. "As you have helped me, so I shall help you," it said. "Take this pebble. If ever you are in danger, throw it over your shoulder."

Elena put the pebble in her pocket and ran on into the dark forest, where the trees grow so close together that not a speck of sunshine can get through them. Soon she came to a clearing, and there she saw Baba Yaga's hut, which stands on three giant hens' legs and can move about when it likes. The black geese were roosting on the roof of the hut, a kettle was boiling on the fire, and Baba Yaga was asleep inside, snoring through her long nose. Near her on the floor sat Elena's little brother, playing with some bones.

Elena crept into the hut and picked up her brother. But as she ran away into the forest, the black geese saw her. They began to honk and to clap their wings, and Baba Yaga woke up.

"Stop, thief!" she screamed. "Bring back my dinner!"

Elena did not stop, or answer the witch, but hurried on with her little brother in her arms; and Baba Yaga came out of her hut and started after them on her long bony legs.

Elena could not run very fast, because her brother was too heavy. When she came out of the forest and looked back, she saw that the witch was gaining on them. What could she do? Suddenly she remembered what the fish had said, so she reached into her pocket and threw the shell over her shoulder.

At once a broad lake appeared behind her. It was too large for Baba Yaga to go around it, so she squatted down by the edge and began to drink. She drank so fast that the water began to sink at once, and it was

not long before she had drunk up the whole lake. Then she ran on.

Elena looked back and saw that the lake was gone and that Baba Yaga was gaining on them again. She remembered what the squirrel had said, reached into her pocket, and threw the walnut over her shoulder.

At once a thick grove of trees sprang up behind her. They grew so close together that Baba Yaga could not get through. So she began to chew up the trees with her sharp teeth. She ate so fast that in a few minutes she had eaten up the whole grove of trees. Then she ran on.

Elena looked back again and saw that the trees were gone and the witch was coming after her again, so close that she could hear her gnashing her long teeth and see her reaching out her bony arms to grab them. She felt in her pocket and threw the pebble over her shoulder.

Instantly a stony mountain sprang up behind her, so tall that its top was lost in the clouds. Baba Yaga could not eat it or drink it; and she could not get over it. So she had to go back into the forest, growling and cursing.

As for Elena, she went on to her village and was safe at home playing with her little brother when her father and mother got back from market with the sugar buns.

BY PENELOPE LIVELY

ARIAN AND SIMON WERE SENT TO BED EARLY ON THE DAY THAT THE BROWN FAMILY MOVED HOUSE. By then everyone had lost their temper with everyone else; the cat had been sick on the living room carpet; the dog had run away twice. If you have ever moved you will know what kind of a day it had been. Suitcases, boxes, and newspaper all over the place . . . sandwiches instead of proper meals . . . the kettle lost and a wardrobe stuck on the stairs and Mrs. Brown's favorite vase broken. There was bread and baked beans for supper, the television wouldn't work, and the water wasn't hot, so when all was said and done the children didn't object too violently to being sent off to bed. They'd had enough, too. They had one last argument about who was going to sleep by the window, put on their pajamas, got into bed, switched off the lights . . . and it was at that point that the ghost came out of the bottom drawer of the chest of drawers.

It oozed out, a gray cloudy shape about three feet long smelling faintly of smoke, sat down on a chair, and began to hum to itself. It looked like a bundle of sheets and blankets, except that it was not solid: You could see, quite clearly, the cushion on the chair beneath it.

Marian gave a shriek. "That's a ghost!"

"Oh, be quiet, dear," said the ghost. "That noise goes right through my head. And it's not nice to call people names." It took out a ball of wool and some needles and began to knit.

What would you have done? Well, yes—Simon and Marian did just that, and I'm sure you can imagine what happened. You try telling your mother that you can't get to sleep because there's a ghost sitting in the room clacking its knitting needles and humming. Mrs. Brown said the kind of things she could be expected to say, and the ghost continued sitting there knitting and humming, and Mrs. Brown went out, banging the door and saying threatening things about if there's so much as another word from either of you . . .

"She can't see it," said Marian to Simon.

" 'Course not, dear," said the ghost. "It's the kiddies I'm here for. I sure love kiddies. We're going to be such good friends."

"Go away!" yelled Simon. "This is our house now!"

"No it isn't," said the ghost smugly. "I've been here more than a hundred years. I've seen plenty of families come and go. Go to bed now. Be good children."

The children glared at it and buried themselves under the covers. And eventually, they slept.

The next night it was there again. This time it was smoking a long white pipe and reading a newspaper dated 1842. Beside it was a second gray cloudy shape. "Hello, dearies," said the ghost. "Say how do you do to my auntie Edna."

"She can't come here, too," wailed Marian.

"Oh yes she can," said the ghost. "Auntie always comes here in August. She likes a change."

Auntie Edna was even worse than the first ghost. She sucked peppermint drops that smelled so strong that Mrs. Brown, when she came to kiss the children good night, looked suspiciously under their pillows. She also

sang hymns in a loud squeaky voice. The children lay there groaning and the ghosts sang and rustled the newspapers and ate peppermints.

The next night there were three of them. "Meet Uncle Charlie!" said the first ghost. The children groaned.

"And Jip," said the ghost. "Here, Jip, good dog—come and say hello to the kiddies." A large gray dog that you could see straight through came out from under the bed, wagging its tail. The cat, who had been curled up beside Marian's feet (it was supposed to sleep in the kitchen, but there are always ways for a resourceful cat to get what it wants), gave a howl and shot on top of the wardrobe, where it sat spitting. The dog lay down in the middle of the rug and began scratching itself vigorously—it had ghost fleas!

Uncle Charlie was unbearable. He had a loud cough that kept going off like a machine gun, and he told the longest, most pointless stories the children had ever heard. He said he, too, loved kiddies and he knew kiddies loved stories. In the middle of the seventh story the children went to sleep out of sheer boredom.

The following week the ghosts left the bedroom and were to be found all over the house. The children had no peace at all. They'd be quietly doing their homework, and all of a sudden Auntie Edna would be breathing down their necks reciting math problems. The original ghost could usually be found sitting on top of the television with his legs in front of the picture. Uncle Charlie told his stories all through the best programs, and the dog lay permanently at the top of the stairs. The Browns' cat became quite hysterical, refused to eat, and went to live on the top shelf of the kitchen dresser.

Something had to be done. Marian and Simon were also beginning to show the effects; their mother decided they looked tired and brought them sticky brown vitamins from the drugstore to help them regain their energy. "It's the ghosts!" wailed the children. "We don't need vitamins!" Their mother said that she didn't want to hear another word of this silly nonsense about ghosts. Auntie Edna, who was sitting smirking on the other side of the kitchen table at that very moment, nodded vigorously and took out a small bag of peppermint candies, which she sucked noisily.

"We've got to get them to go and live somewhere else," said Marian. But where, that was the problem, and how? It was then that they had a bright idea. On Sunday the Browns were all going to see their uncle, who was rather rich and lived alone in a big house with thick carpets everywhere and empty rooms and the biggest color television you ever saw. Plenty of room for ghosts.

They were very sneaky. They suggested to the ghosts that they might like a drive in the country. At first, the ghosts said that they were quite comfortable where they were, thank you, and they didn't like driving around in modern cars, not at their time of life. But then Auntie Edna remembered that she liked looking at the pretty flowers and the trees and finally they agreed to give it a try. They sat in a row crouched up behind the backseat of the car. Mrs. Brown kept asking why there was such a strong smell of peppermint, and Mr. Brown kept roaring at Simon and Marian to keep still while he was driving. The fact was that the ghosts were shoving them; it was like being nudged by three cold, damp bedsheets. And the ghost dog, who had come along, too, of course, was carsick.

When they got to Uncle Dick's the ghosts came in and had a look round. They liked the expensive carpets and the enormous television. They slid in and out of the closets and walked through the doors and the walls and sent Uncle Dick's parakeets into a bad state from which they have never recovered. Nice place, they said, nice and comfy.

"Why not stay here?" said Simon, in an offhand tone.

"Couldn't do that," said the ghosts firmly. "No kiddies. Dull. We like a place with a bit of life to it." And they piled back into the car and sang songs all the way home to the Browns' house. They also ate toast. There were real toast crumbs on the floor, and the children got the blame.

Simon and Marian were in despair. The ruder they were to the ghosts the more the ghosts liked it. "Disrespectful!" they said indulgently. "What a disrespectful little pair of kiddies! There, now . . . come and give Uncle a kiss." The children weren't even safe in the bathtub. One or another of the ghosts would come and sit on the faucets and talk to them. Uncle Charlie had produced a harmonica and played the same tune over and over again; it was quite annoying. The children went around with their hands over their ears. Mrs. Brown took them to the doctor to find out if there was something wrong with their hearing. The children knew better than to say anything to the doctor about the ghosts. It was pointless saying anything to anyone.

I don't know what would have happened if Mrs. Brown hadn't happened to make friends with Mrs. Walker from down the road. Mrs. Walker had twin babies, and one day she brought the babies along for tea.

Now, one baby is bad enough. Two babies are trouble in a big way. These babies created pandemonium. When they weren't both howling, they were crawling around the floor pulling the tablecloths off the tables or hitting their heads on the chairs and hauling the books out of the bookcases. They threw their food all over the kitchen and flung cups of milk on the floor. Their mother mopped up after them and every time she tried to have a conversation with Mrs. Brown the babies bawled in chorus so that no one could hear a word.

In the middle of this the ghosts appeared. One baby was yelling its head off, and the other was gluing pieces of chewed-up bread onto the front of the television. The ghosts swooped down on them with happy cries. "Oh!" they trilled. "Bless their little hearts. Give Auntie a smile then." And the babies stopped in midhowl and gazed at the ghosts. The ghosts cooed at the babies, and the babies cooed at the ghosts. The ghosts chattered to the babies and sang them songs, and the babies chattered back and were as good as gold for the next hour, and their mother had the first uninterrupted conversation she'd had in weeks. When they left, the ghosts stood in a row at the window, waving.

Simon and Marian knew when to seize an opportunity. That evening they had a talk with the ghosts. At first the ghosts raised objections. They didn't like the idea of moving, they said; you got set in your ways at their age; Auntie Edna thought that a strange house would be the death of her.

The children talked about the babies relentlessly.

And the next day they led the ghosts down the road, followed by the ghost dog, and into the Walkers' house. Mrs. Walker doesn't know to this day why the babies, who had been screaming for the last half hour, suddenly stopped and broke into great smiles. And she had never understood why, from that day forth, the babies became the most tranquil, quiet, good-natured babies in the area. The ghosts kept the babies amused from morning to night. The babies thrived; the ghosts were happy; the ghost dog, who was actually a female, settled down so well that she had puppies, which is one of the most surprising aspects of the whole business. The Brown children heaved a sigh of relief and got back to normal life. The babies, though, I have to tell you, grew up somewhat strange.

 ITH

CREAKS

AND HOWLS

DUFFY'S JACKET

BY BRUCE COVILLE

I F MY COUSIN DUFFY HAD THE BRAINS OF A TURNIP IT NEVER WOULD HAVE HAPPENED. But as far as I'm concerned, Duffy makes a turnip look bright. My mother disagrees. According to her, Duffy is actually very bright. She claims the reason he's so scatterbrained is that he's too busy being brilliant inside his own head to remember everyday things. Maybe. But hanging around with Duffy means you spend a lot of time saying, "Your glasses, Duffy," or "Your coat, Duffy," or—well, you get the idea: a lot of three-word sentences that start with "Your" and end with "Duffy" and have words like "book," "radio," "wallet," or whatever it is he's just put down and left behind, stuck in the middle.

Me, I think turnips are brighter.

But since Duffy's my cousin, and since my mother and her sister are both single parents, we tend to do a lot of things together—like camping, which is how we got into the mess I want to tell you about.

Personally, I thought camping was a big mistake. But since Mom and Aunt Elise are raising the three of us—me, Duffy, and my little sister, Marie—on their own, they're convinced they have to do man stuff with us every once in a while. I think they read some kind of book that said me and Duffy would come out weird if they don't. You can take him camping all you want. It ain't gonna make Duffy normal.

Anyway, the fact that our mothers were getting wound up to do something fatherly, combined with the fact that Aunt Elise's boss had a friend who had a friend who said we could use his cabin, added up to the five of us bouncing along this horrible dirt road late one Friday in October.

It was late because we had lost an hour going back to get Duffy's suitcase. I suppose it wasn't actually Duffy's fault. No one remembered to say, "Your suitcase, Duffy," so he couldn't really have been expected to remember it.

"Oh, Elise," cried my mother, as we got deeper into the woods. "Aren't the leaves beautiful?"

That's why it doesn't make sense for them to try to do man stuff with us. If it had been our fathers, they would have been drinking beer and burping and maybe telling dirty stories, instead of talking about the leaves. So why try to fake it?

Anyway, we get to this cabin, which is about eighteen million miles from nowhere, and to my surprise, it's not a cabin at all. It's a house. A big house.

"Oh my," said my mother as we pulled into the driveway.

"Isn't it great?" chirped Aunt Elise. "It's almost a hundred years old, back from the time when they used to build big hunting lodges up here. It's the only one in the area still standing. Horace said he hasn't been able to get up here in some time. That's why he was glad to let us use it. He said it would be good to have someone go in and air the place out."

Leave it to Aunt Elise. This place didn't need airing our—it needed fumigating. I never saw so many spiderwebs in my life. From the sounds we heard coming from the walls, the mice seemed to have made it a population center. We found a total of two working lightbulbs: one in the kitchen and one in the dining room, which was paneled with dark wood and had a big stone fireplace at one end.

"Oh my," said my mother again.

Duffy, who's allergic to about fifteen different things, started to sneeze.

"Isn't it charming?" said Aunt Elise hopefully.

No one answered her.

Four hours later we had managed to get three bedrooms clean enough to sleep in without getting the heebie-jeebies—one for Mom and Aunt Elise, one for Marie, and one for me and Duffy. After a supper of beans and franks we hit the hay, which I think is what our mattresses were stuffed with. As I was drifting off, which took about thirty seconds, it occurred to me that four hours of housework wasn't all that much of a man thing, something it might be useful to remember the next time Mom got one of these plans into her head.

Things looked better in the morning when we went outside and found a stream where we could go wading. ("Your sneakers, Duffy.")

Later we went back and started poking around the house, which really was enormous.

That was when things started getting a little spooky. In the room next to ours I found a message scrawled on the wall. BEWARE THE SENTINEL, it said in big black letters.

When I showed Mom and Aunt Elise, they said it was just a joke and got mad at me for frightening Marie.

Marie wasn't the only one who was frightened.

We decided to go out for another walk. ("Your lunch, Duffy.") We went deep into the woods, following a faint trail that kept threatening to disappear but never actually faded away altogether. It was a hot day, even in the deep woods, and after a while we decided to take off our coats.

When we got back and Duffy didn't have his jacket, did they get mad at him? My mother actually had the nerve to say, "Why didn't you remind him? You know he forgets things like that."

What do I look like, a walking memo pad?

Anyway, I had other things on my mind—like the fact that I was convinced someone had been following us out of the woods.

I tried to tell my mother about it, but first she said I was being ridiculous, and then she accused me of trying to sabotage the trip.

So I shut up. But I was pretty nervous, especially when Mom and Elise announced that they were going into town—which was twenty miles away—to pick up some supplies (like lightbulbs).

"You kids will be fine on your own," said Mom cheerfully. "You can make popcorn and play Monopoly. And there's enough soda here for you to make yourselves sick on."

And with that they were gone.

It got dark.

We played Monopoly.

They didn't come back. That didn't surprise me. Since Duffy and I were both fifteen they felt it was okay to leave us on our own, and Mom had warned us they might decide to have dinner at the little inn we had seen on the way up.

But I would have been happier if they had been there.

Especially when something started scratching on the door.

"What was that?" said Marie.

"What was what?" asked Duffy.

"That!" she said, and this time I heard it, too. My stomach rolled over, and the skin at the back of my neck started to prickle.

"Maybe it's the Sentinel!" I hissed.

"Andrew!" yelled Marie. "Mom told you not to say that."

"She said not to try to scare you," I said. "I'm not. *I'm scared!* I told you I heard something following us in the woods today."

Scratch, scratch.

"But you said it stopped," said Duffy. "So how would it know where we are now?"

"I don't know. I don't know what it is. Maybe it tracked us, like a bloodhound."

Scratch, scratch.

"Don't bloodhounds have to have something to give them a scent?" asked Marie. "Like a piece of clothing . . . or—"

We both looked at Duffy.

"Your jacket, Duffy!"

Duffy turned white.

"That's silly," he said after a moment.

"There's something at the door," I said frantically. "Maybe it's been lurking around all day, waiting for our mothers to leave. Maybe it's been waiting for someone to come back here."

Scratch, scratch.

"I don't believe it," said Duffy. "It's just the wind moving a branch. I'll prove it."

He got up and headed for the door. But he didn't open it. Instead he peeked through the window next to it. When he turned back, his eyes looked as big as the hard-boiled eggs we had eaten for supper.

"There's something out there!" he hissed. *"Something big!"*

"I told you," I cried. "Oh, I knew there was something there."

"Andrew, are you doing this just to scare me?" said Marie. "Because if you are—"

Scratch, scratch.

"Come on," I said, grabbing her by the hand. "Let's get out of here."

I started to lead her up the stairs.

"Not there!" said Duffy. "If we go up there we'll be trapped."

"You're right," I said. "Let's go out the back way!"

The thought of going outside scared the daylights out of me. But at least out there we would have somewhere to run. Inside—well, who knew what might happen if the thing found us inside.

We went into the kitchen.

I heard the front door open.

"Let's get out of here!" I hissed.

We scooted out the back door. "What now?" I wondered, looking around frantically.

"The barn," whispered Duffy. "We can hide in the barn."

"Good idea," I said. Holding Marie by the hand, I led the way to the barn. But the door was held shut by a huge padlock.

The wind was blowing harder, but not hard enough to hide the sound of the back door of the house opening and slamming shut.

"Quick!" I whispered. "It knows we're out here. Let's sneak around front. It will never expect us to go back into the house."

Duffy and Marie followed me as I led them behind a hedge. I caught a glimpse of something heading toward the barn and swallowed nervously. It was big. Very big.

"I'm scared," whispered Marie.

"Shhhh!" I hissed. "We can't let it know where we are."

We slipped through the front door. We locked it, just like people always do in the movies, though what good that would do I couldn't figure, since if something really wanted to get at us it would just break the window and come in.

"Upstairs," I whispered.

We tiptoed up the stairs. Once we were in our bedroom, I thought we were safe. Crawling over the floor, I raised my head just enough to peek out the window. My heart almost stopped. Standing in the moonlight was an enormous manlike creature. It had a scrap of cloth in its hands. It was looking around—looking for us. I saw it lift its head and sniff the wind. To my horror, it started back toward the house.

"It's coming back!" I yelped, more frightened than ever.

"How does it know where we are?" asked Marie.

But I knew how. It had Duffy's jacket. It was tracking us down, like some giant bloodhound.

We huddled together in the middle of the room, trying to think of what to do.

A minute later we heard it.

Scratch, scratch.

None of us moved.

Scratch, scratch.

We stopped breathing, then jumped up in alarm at a terrible crashing sound.

The door was down.

We hunched back against the wall as heavy footsteps came clomping up the stairs.

I wondered what our mothers would think when they got back. Would they find our bodies? Or would there be nothing left of us at all?

Thump. Thump. Thump.

It was getting closer.

Thump. Thump. Thump.

It was outside the door.

Knock. Knock.

"Don't answer!" hissed Duffy.

Like I said, he doesn't have the brains of a turnip.

It didn't matter. The door wasn't locked. It came swinging open. In the shaft of light I saw a huge figure. The Sentinel of the Woods! It

had to be. I thought I was going to die.

The figure stepped into the room. Its head nearly touched the ceiling.

Marie squeezed against my side tighter than a tick in a dog's ear.

The huge creature sniffed the air. It turned in our direction. Its eyes seemed to glow. Moonlight glittered on its fangs.

Slowly the Sentinel raised its arm. I could see Duffy's jacket dangling from its fingertips.

And then it spoke.

"You forgot your jacket, stupid."

It threw the jacket at Duffy, turned around, and stomped down the stairs.

Which is why, I suppose, no one has had to remind Duffy to remember his jacket, or his glasses, or his math book, for at least a year now.

After all, when you leave stuff lying around, you never can be sure just who might bring it back.

BY PHYLLIS MACLENNAN

MISS AGNES PATTERSON'S FIFTH-GRADE CLASS SAT RIGID UNDER THE GORGON EYE OF THEIR TEACHER, waiting to be programmed into the next item on their tightly organized schedule.

Motionless, backs straight, hands neatly folded on their desks, faces careful masks of respectful submission, they seemed unaware that it was the last day before Easter vacation, with school almost out and spring waiting for them beyond the open windows. The trees now lightly smudged with pink, the call of carefree birds, the rich warm smell of the moist earth and new growing things seemed to hold no charm for them. Not one so much as glanced outside. Apart from discipline, there was something on the windowsill that they could not bear to look at: an empty hamster cage.

The cage awaited no new occupant. It was simply there, to remind them of their failure in their nature study project—a frippery of modern education that Miss Patterson had never quite approved of. The committee appointed to care for the little beast had forgotten to take it home with them over the Christmas vacation, and their teacher, seeing in this oversight a heaven-sent opportunity for a stern lesson on Responsibility, had left the animal to the fate its thoughtless guardians had abandoned it to. When they came back after their holiday, they found it dead, lying on its back, eyes closed, mouth open, stiff and cold. Miss Patterson's vivid description of the torments the hamster must have suffered as it starved and thirsted to death had left most of the children in hysterical tears. One thing was sure: None of them would turn his or her eyes in the direction of that reproaching cage, no matter what marvelous events might transpire beyond the window. They sat, subdued, fully under control. When their teacher cracked the whip, they would jump.

All except Corinna.

Defiant little witch Corinna! She sat in the corner like a cat wandered in on a whim, watching what went on with a cat's inscrutable smoldering stare, or turning her attention inward to mysterious thoughts of her own. She had a reputation as a troublemaker. She had been transferred from room to room all year as teacher after teacher refused to cope with her. Her parents had been called, but they refused to discuss the problem like good parents. They said that their daughter went to school because the law required it, and the law made her behave, if it could. It was no concern of theirs.

She had been in Miss Patterson's class for little more than a week, and though she had done nothing overt, in her mere presence the group was beginning to disintegrate. The children were restless, uneasy, like sheep who scent the wolf. Her contempt for the activities in which they spent their days was obvious. She refused to answer questions when called on, did no homework, turned in blank papers—and with her example before them, the others were beginning, ever so slightly, to get out of hand.

Miss Patterson was not disturbed. She had been dealing with troublemakers for twenty years, and she knew how to break them. Her methods were not subtle, but they were effective, and Corinna had put her most effective weapon to her hand by turning in an arithmetic test with nothing on it but her name. Miss Patterson returned the tests and addressed her pupils in a voice like honey on a razor's edge.

"Elephants have giant brains, and so all those who had perfect papers are elephants. Stand up, elephants, so we can see you. . . . My, we have a lot of elephants, haven't we? . . . Mice have little brains and don't pay attention, and so they make mistakes, but they can squeeze by. Stand up mice. . . . Fleas are little tiny parasites with no brains at all. They're really stupid. We don't have any fleas in our class, do we? . . . Oh, we do have one! Corinna didn't get one single answer on this test! She couldn't answer any of the questions! Stand up, Corinna. You must be a very tiny flea indeed!"

She smiled triumphantly and looked to see Corinna crushed.

"If I'm a flea, you're an old bat."

It was unthinkable that such impertinence could be. Stunned, helplessly conscious of her mouth gone slack, her burning face, Miss Patterson sat paralyzed. Transfixed by Corinna's eyes, fierce and yellow and soulless as a hawk's, she knew—how could she not have known before? How could she not have seen what she now saw so clearly? This was no child like other children.

"You are a bat," Corinna repeated ominously, her witch's eyes grown huge and luminous. She glided forward, reached the desk, and slid around it like a snake. Behind her, suddenly aware, bonded with her, strengthening her with their united wills, the children converged on their teacher. They gathered around her desk, all of them staring. . . .

Did they grow larger? Was it she who shrank? They loomed above her, glaring down with savage joy.

Agnes Patterson fluttered off her chair and scuttled away between their feet, screaming for help in a voice too shrill for human ears to hear. The children, shrieking their triumph, raced after her, chivvying her from corner to corner, striking at her as she dove past them. Help came at last, brought by the pandemonium in the room—Mr. Morgan from across the hall.

"What's going on here!"

"It's our bat!" Corinna shouted. "Our nature study bat! It got away!"

"Yes, yes!" the children chorused. "We're trying to catch it and put it back in the cage!"

"Where's Miss Patterson? She should have told me she was stepping out so I could cover her . . . never mind." He pulled off his jacket and in one deft swoop captured the hysterically chittering creature and

stuffed it into the cage. He closed its door and glanced at his watch. "It's nearly time for dismissal. You kids sit quiet. I'll be keeping an eye on you from my room."

They took their places and sat until the bell rang. They said nothing aloud, but gleeful eyes met and giggles were muffled behind their hands as they gathered their things and left silently, in impeccable order, attracting no attention to themselves and their unsupervised classroom. Corinna waited until the others had gone. She came then and stood in front of the cage. The captive shrank still farther back, but there was no move to harm her.

"Good-bye, Miss Patterson," Corinna whispered. "Have a nice vacation."

She tiptoed out and closed the door behind her.

THE WITCH WHO WAS AFRAID OF WITCHES

FROM THE BOOK BY ALICE LOW

WENDY WAS THE YOUNGEST WITCH IN HER FAMILY. She had the weakest witch power. And she was afraid of witches. Older, bossy, mean witches like her two sisters.

Her oldest sister *knew* everything. She knew where to get the best sassafras wood for broomsticks. She knew where to get the best frogs' tongues for witches' brew. And she knew where to get the best books for witches' spells.

"Take me with you," Wendy begged when her oldest sister was going to the sassafras grove.

But her oldest sister always said, "You're too young. You don't even have the right kind of wood in your broomstick. No wonder you can hardly take off. You'll never learn. Really, Wendy, you don't know anything."

Wendy wanted to say, "Of course I don't. How can I learn if you won't show me?"

But she was afraid to talk back to her oldest sister.

Her middle sister knew how to *do* everything best. She could fly the fastest of any witch in the valley. She could cackle the loudest. When she cackled, *"Heh, heh, heh. I'll get you,"* she really got you.

And she could say the spells in the most frightening voice, to make them work the best.

"Teach me how to say spells in that frightening voice," Wendy begged.

But her middle sister always said, "Really, Wendy, your voice is too weak. You don't even know how to cackle."

Wendy didn't even try to learn the spells. What good would it do if she didn't have a frightening voice?

At night, her sisters had parties.

Wendy would sit at the top of the stairs, listening to the loud cackles of witch laughter. How she wished she could join in!

When one of her sisters saw her she would shout, "Spying, eh? Off with you. It's past your bedtime."

And Wendy would creep into her cold bed, hugging her broomstick.

She was afraid of the dark. Afraid of witches.

Sometimes she tried to make up a spell and put it on her sisters.

But she couldn't think of anything. She needed her sisters to tell her the right words.

"At least I have *you*," she said to her broomstick. "You give me a little witch power."

Then, the day before Halloween, she lost her broomstick.

Neither of her sisters would give her another. "Serves you right," they said.

She felt lost without it. Now she had no witch power at all.

On Halloween night, her sisters said, "We are going to the city where there are more people to scare."

"Take me with you," Wendy said. "Please."

"Really, Wendy, how can you come with us when you have no broomstick?" her oldest sister said.

"Can't I ride with you on yours?" Wendy asked.

"Of course not. You would make it too heavy. Stay here, and don't let anyone in. All those trick-or-treaters eat our candy and squirt shaving cream on the rug. Remember, don't let them in."

Wendy wasn't afraid of trick-or-treaters. She was much more afraid of witches.

"Turn off the lights, lock the door, and put out the fire," her oldest sister said. "It will look like nobody is home."

Wendy did as they said.

Then she sat in the dark, shivering. If only she had her broomstick for company.

Soon there was a knock on the door.

"Trick or treat," shouted a voice.

Wendy opened the window and called out, "There's nobody home."

"You're home," said a small ghost on the doorstep.

"Well, I'm nobody," Wendy said.

"Is that what you are for Halloween?" asked the ghost. "Are you nobody?"

"Yes," Wendy said. "But I'm dressed as a witch."

"Well, why don't you come trick-or-treating with me?" asked the ghost. "My best friend, Billy, went trick-or-treating with his other best friend, who doesn't like me. Let's follow them and scare them."

"That sounds good to me," Wendy said. "Though I'm not very good at scaring people. Mostly, *I'm* scared of witches."

"Oh, you'll catch on," said the ghost. "You just go *woo, woo, woo.*"

"That's how *ghosts* go," Wendy said. "Witches cackle. Like this: *Heh, heh, heh. I'll get you.*"

"Very good," said the ghost. "You sound like a real witch."

"Do I?" Wendy said. "I never thought I could cackle before. But I can't be a real witch without a broomstick. I lost mine."

"Oh, if that's all you need, we have an old one at home. Come on."

They walked up a long path to the ghost's house.

The ghost's mother gave Wendy hot chocolate and a candied apple and a broomstick.

Wendy thought it would be nice to stay there all evening, instead of flying around scaring people.

But the ghost said, "Get on. Let's see you ride."

"I'm not any good at riding broomsticks," Wendy said, afraid to try. "I have no witch power."

"Take the broomstick anyway," said the ghost.

So Wendy took the broomstick, but she didn't sit on it. This old kitchen broomstick wouldn't give her any witch power.

"Go on," said the ghost. "Sit on it. It's fun."

"Okay," Wendy said. After all, the ghost didn't expect her to do anything but pretend and have fun.

She sat on the broomstick and said, *"Heh, heh, heh. I'll get you."* Then she gave a little jump.

She took off so fast she hit the ceiling and fell down.

The ghost was amazed. So was the ghost's mother.

"That must be a magic broomstick," said the ghost. "Here, let me try it."

The ghost got on and said, *"Heh, heh, heh. I'll get you."* Then he gave a little jump.

But nothing happened.

"Darn it. It doesn't work," said the ghost.

"I'll try it," said the ghost's mother.

She sat on it and cackled and gave a little jump. But nothing happened again. They were both very disappointed.

"I'll try it again," Wendy said.

Again, she took off easily. But this time, she zoomed around and around before she landed.

"I guess I do have a little witch power," she said. "I never thought so before. Except I don't know any spells."

"Then make one up," said the ghost. "You're magic."

That made a really good spell pop into Wendy's head. She said it in a frightening voice.

Frogs and lizards
Toads and newts
Rubbers, raincoats
Hiking boots.
Turn this ghost
Into a witch.
Presto, change-o
Make a switch.

The ghost's robes turned black.

"Great!" said the ghost. "I wanted to be a witch, but we didn't have any black sheets. But I need a pointed hat."

"Oh, that's easy," Wendy said. "I don't even have to think about that one."

Stew and brew
And cat and bat.
Give this witch
A pointed hat.

"Great!" said the new witch, touching the pointed hat on his head. "Now let's fly out the window."

"Be careful," said the new witch's mother. "Don't fly too fast."

"We won't," they called from the broomstick as they flew out, with Wendy steering.

First they swooped over trees and made the leaves fall off. Next they swooped over cars and scared the drivers. Then they swooped into the party where Billy and his best friend were ducking for apples.

Billy and his best friend were so scared, they ran home crying.

When the clock struck midnight, Wendy said, "I'd better fly you home."

"I want to come home with you and keep on being a witch," said the new witch. "You *are* a real witch, aren't you?"

"Yes, I am a real witch," Wendy said. "With my own witch power. I just found that out, and you helped. But I have to turn you back into a ghost and take you home. Your mother would miss you."

Broiled figs
And toasted toast.
Turn this witch
Back to a ghost.

The new witch became a ghost again, in his own kitchen.

The ghost's mother let Wendy keep the broomstick.

"Thanks a lot," Wendy said. "See you next Halloween."

And she flew home and went to sleep without worrying about witches. She wasn't afraid of witches anymore.

RAP! RAP! RAP!

RETOLD BY JEANNE B. HARDENDORFF

ON A VERY DARK AND MOONLESS NIGHT LAST DECEMBER, Reginald Ewing Peabody was driving his car very slowly and most carefully on that particular road in the southwest corner of the county that goes by the three houses that have been deserted for so many years.

He was driving very slowly for he was having trouble seeing the road. His headlights were very dim and it was obvious to Reginald Ewing Peabody that something was drastically wrong with the battery of his car. That road goes uphill and downhill with great monotony when it isn't curving first this way and that way. The road is narrow and the hedges have grown tall and close to the road—all of which add to the difficulties of driving along that particular road late at night.

Reginald Ewing Peabody was on that road as it was a shorter route than the main highway to the house where he was expected to spend the night. He had passed two of those deserted houses a long way back, it seemed to him, and he had not passed nor seen another car for miles.

His headlights were growing dimmer and dimmer. The night was growing darker and darker. His car had just reached the crest of a hill when there was a flash of lightning followed by the pelting of rain against the windshield. At this onslaught of nature the battery, which Reginald Ewing Peabody had begun to think of as having human characteristics (he had been talking to it, urging it along, pleading and

cajoling with it not to abandon him in his need), took that very instant to give up the ghost—it went completely dead.

And there was Reginald Ewing Peabody, miles from any village. He had seen the outline of a house over to his left when a flash of lightning lessened the blackness of the night for a moment.

He needed some shelter from the storm—for his car was old and far from waterproof. He thought that it was possible that there might be someone living in that house and that he might be able to telephone the nearest garage. So he buttoned his slicker, turned up the collar, and made a run for the house.

At the road there was a gate that creaked and moaned as he opened and shut it. The bricks in the walk were slippery with the rain and seemed to be covered with moss as though no one had walked on them for quite some time. But he thought he had noticed a light upstairs.

He knocked on the door. But all he heard was the echo of his knock. So he knocked again. No one seemed to be coming to answer the door.

He tried the doorknob. It turned in his hand and the door opened. Reginald Ewing Peabody called out, "Anyone home?"

No answer. The only sound he heard was a faint *rap, rap, rap.* And the sound was coming from upstairs.

So Reginald Ewing Peabody stepped into the front hall. He called again, "Anyone home?"

No answer. Only the sound *rap, rap, rap,* and it was definitely coming from upstairs. Reginald Ewing Peabody lit a match so that he could see to climb the stairs. The match burned until he reached the upstairs landing and then it went out.

He could hear the *rap, rap, rap,* but now it was louder. So he lit another match, and he went down the hall toward the sound.

Rap, rap, rap. The sound led Reginald Ewing Peabody past one door, past a second door, until he came to a third door.

The sound was coming from behind that third door.

Rap, rap, rap.

Reginald Ewing Peabody opened the door. Behind the door were some stairs. The stairs led up to the attic. So he lit another match.

He climbed the attic steps and all the time the *rap, rap, rap* was getting louder and louder.

Reginald Ewing Peabody stepped onto the attic floor. He looked all around the attic. He could hear the rapping sound. At last he noticed a

door. The rapping sound was coming from behind that door.

He had taken three steps toward the door, when his match burnt out, so he lit another match.

Rap, rap, rap, the sound was getting louder.

Reginald Ewing Peabody reached the door and he opened it.

Rap! Rap! Rap!

He looked in the closet.

Rap! Rap! Rap!

On the shelf of the closet was a box. The rapping sound was coming from the box.

Reginald Ewing Peabody opened the box. Inside was a roll of wrapping paper.

GOTCHA!

I'M COMING UP THE STAIRS

AN ENGLISH FOLKTALE
RETOLD BY WENDY WAX

TILLY COULD BARELY WAIT FOR HER DAD'S STATION WAGON TO PULL UP IN THE DRIVEWAY. That's because her older brother Herbie was in the car. Herbie had been away all summer at sleep-away camp, and Tilly had to spend a boring summer without him. Tilly couldn't wait to hear her brother's camp stories about other campers, his counselors, and the activities he had signed up for. After all, she had to know what to expect next year when she was old enough to go, too.

But when Herbie got home, all he wanted to do was sleep. When Tilly asked why he was so tired, he said it was because he and his bunkmates stayed up all night telling spooky tales about the Creep Man.

"Tell me about the Creep Man," begged Tilly. "Tell me, tell me."

"It'll scare you, Tilly," Herbie said.

"No it won't," said his sister. "I'm bigger now."

"Mom and Dad won't like it," said Herbie.

"They're not home."

Finally, Herbie agreed to tell Tilly about the Creep Man who had been haunting Camp Bugwood for years. He told her everything he knew—though most of it was still vague. The Creep Man lived on children's ear wax, sharpened his teeth on small fingernails, and liked to cuddle up in campers' sleeping bags—even though he wasn't invited. Every year, the Creep Man followed one kid home from camp and hung

out in his or her house all winter. Rumor had it that the boy the Creep Man went home with at the end of last summer didn't come back to camp—even though he said he was coming back for sure.

"Wh-who did the Creep Man go home with this year?" Tilly asked, suddenly a little shaky. She was sorry she had made her brother tell her about the Creep Man.

But her brother didn't answer. He had fallen fast asleep on the couch, and when Herbie was asleep, no one could wake him.

Tilly spent the rest of the day trying to forget about the Creep Man. But everywhere she looked or went or thought about reminded her of him. She couldn't wait for her parents to get home but it got later and later. When they didn't come home for dinner, she began to get worried—and hungry. Finally, she fixed herself a peanut butter and jelly sandwich and a glass of chocolate milk, ate quickly, and hurried upstairs to her room, closing her door of course. "Just in case," she told herself unconvincingly. Then she put on her pajamas and, without brushing her teeth, got into bed.

CREAK!

Tilly jumped up and grabbed Freddy the Teddy from her dresser. She'd been trying to give up her "babyish" habit of sleeping with him, but this . . .

CREAK!

. . . was a special case!

Suddenly she heard a soft voice say, "Tilly, I'm on the second step."

Tilly buried her head in Freddy the Teddy's soft stomach. "This must be a dream," she told herself.

But the next CREAK! was louder than the others. "Tilly, I'm on the third step."

By this time, Tilly was shaking like she never had before. She pulled the covers up over both her and Freddy the Teddy's head.

"Tilly, I'm on the fourth step."

"Tilly, I'm on the fifth step." The voice was getting louder and louder.

Where were her parents? Tilly would sure tell them off in the morning—that is, if she were still . . .

CREAK! "Tilly, I'm on the sixth step." What could she do now?

"Tilly, I'm in the hall."

The footsteps were softly thudding down the hall toward her room!

"Tilly, I'm at your door."

Cr-ree-eaak. "Tilly, I'm in your bedroom!"

By now, Tilly was grasping Freddy the Teddy so tightly that his ear was beginning to come off. She had never been so terrified in her life. But this was the first Creep Man she had ever encountered. Just then she gasped. The bed had sunk lower!

"Tilly, I'm sitting on your bed."

Tilly would have gone deeper under the covers but she was too afraid to move. She lay there hoping . . .

"I'VE GOT YOU!"

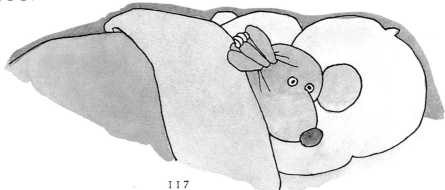

A SCOTTISH FOLKTALE

RETOLD BY WENDY WAX

A WOMAN WAS SITTING AND SPINNING WOOL ONE NIGHT. SHE SAT, AND SHE SPUN, AND SHE WISHED FOR COMPANY.

In came a pair of broad broad feet. Stomped right over to the fireside.

And still she sat, and still she spun, and still she wished for company.

In came a pair of short short legs. Sat themselves down on the broad broad feet.

And still she sat, and still she spun, and still she wished for company.

In came a pair of thick thick knees. Sat themselves down on the thick thick knees.

And still she sat, and still she spun, and still she wished for company.

In came a pair of huge huge hips. Sat themselves down on the short short legs.

And still she sat, and still she spun, and still she wished for company.

In came a wee wee waist. Sat itself down on the huge huge hips.

And still she sat, and still she spun, and still she wished for company.

In came a pair of broad broad shoulders. Sat themselves down on the wee wee waist.

And still she sat, and still she spun, and still she wished for company.

In came a pair of long long arms. Attached themselves to the broad broad shoulders.

And still she sat, and still she spun, and still she wished for company.

In came a pair of huge huge hands. Attached themselves to the long long arms.

And still she sat, and still she spun, and still she wished for company.
In came a small small neck. Sat itself down on the broad broad shoulders.

And still she sat, and still she spun, and still she wished for company.
In came a huge huge head. Sat itself down on the small small neck.

And, at last, the woman spoke:

"How did you get such broad broad feet?"

"MUCH TRAMPING, MUCH TRAMPING." The visitor's voice was gruff.

"How did you get such short short legs?"

"MUCH RUNNING, MUCH RUNNING."

"How did you get such thick thick knees?"

"MUCH PRAYING, MUCH PRAYING."

"How did you get such huge huge hips?"

"MUCH SITTING, MUCH SITTING."

"How did you get such a wee wee waist?"

"MUCH BENDING, MUCH BENDING."

"How did you get such broad broad shoulders?"

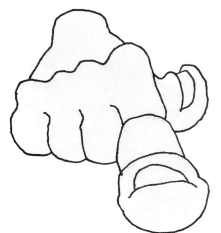

"SWINGING A BAT, SWINGING A BAT."

"How did you get such long long arms?"

"HANGING FROM BRANCHES, HANGING FROM BRANCHES."

"How did you get such huge huge hands?"

"THROWING PUMPKINS, THROWING PUMPKINS."

"How did you get such a small small neck?"

"LOOKING BEHIND ME, LOOKING BEHIND ME."

"How did you get such a huge huge head?"

"LOTS OF BRAINS, LOTS OF BRAINS."

"What did you come for?"

"FOR YOU!"

THE GOLDEN ARM

AN AMERICAN FOLKTALE

RETOLD BY WENDY WAX

THE BEST DAY OF RAY JONES'S LIFE WAS HIS WEDDING DAY. It was not because he married the most beautiful woman in town, nor because he married the friendliest woman in town. Ray Jones's wedding day was the best day of his life because he married a woman who had something no other woman had—a golden arm.

It was about time Ray Jones got married, the townsfolk said. He had gone out with just about every single woman in town. But regardless of their beauty, talents, compatibility, and good sense of humor, none of them could hold Ray's interest for long. But then Isabella moved into the boardinghouse next door.

Ray first noticed Isabella on the morning of her arrival. He'd wakened to the sun streaming through his window, brighter than ever—or so he thought. He jumped out of bed to look out the window, and much to his surprise, he found that the stream of sunlight was really the sun reflecting from a golden arm. The arm rested on an upstairs windowsill, directly across from his own. And the golden arm, he realized, belonged to a beautiful woman with long golden hair. Ray dressed hurriedly and rushed next door to meet his neighbor, who six weeks later became his bride.

Isabella had never loved anyone as much as she loved Ray, and Ray . . . well, Ray had never loved anything as much as he loved Isabella's golden arm. (But Ray acted like it was Isabella he loved.)

As time went on, things changed. Though Ray was still thrilled to be married to a woman with a golden arm, married life didn't really suit him. He could no longer come and go as he pleased, he grew bored having to keep up a conversation, and he longed to have time alone. Ray kept these feelings to himself, though, so as not to cause the neighbors to gossip.

Suddenly and unexpectedly, Isabella died. Everyone in town felt terrible, including Ray Jones—at least he seemed to on the outside. On the inside he was shrieking with joy at the thought of being on his own once again. But before he could fully rejoice, he had some business to take care of.

The night after the funeral, Ray Jones crept through the town in his black clothes with a shovel and a saw. He dug up his wife's body, cut off the golden arm, and reburied her. "Isabella will never know," he told himself. Then, quietly so as not to wake his nosy neighbors, he hurried home.

Ray Jones spent the next day looking for a good place to keep the golden arm. Finding a good hiding place was a bit of a problem. The closet was too dark and dusty, there wasn't much room in the dresser drawers, the kitchen didn't make much sense, and the living room was where visitors came. Finally, he settled for keeping it under his pillow where it would be safe and might even bring good dreams.

That night, Ray was drifting off to sleep when he was awakened by a gust of wind. He got up to close the window and was alarmed to find it was closed—and locked! Where could the wind have come from? Just then he felt a softer breeze, followed by a tall ghostly figure sweeping through the room. It was Isabella—his dead wife! The ghost stalked toward the bed and gazed into Ray's eyes. Ray pretended not to be afraid.

"Why are your cheeks so pale, my d-dear Isabella?" he whispered.

"My red, rosy cheeks have faded away." The ghost moved closer.

"Wh-why are your lips so wh-wh-white?" Ray asked, shrinking back under the covers.

"My red, rosy lips have faded away." The ghost relaxed in a floating position above his bed.

"Wh-what h-have you d-done with your g-g-golden h-hair?" By now Ray was shaking uncontrollably, his head under the covers.

"My golden hair has faded away," said the ghost. A strong breeze blew the covers off of Ray, who began to shiver. The ghost swooped lower, giving Ray a close-up view of wispy shreds that hung down from its right shoulder. "Aren't you going to ask where my golden arm is?"

Ray was silent.

"You loved that golden arm, Ray, didn't you?"

Not wanting to give himself away, Ray asked, "Wh-what h-have y-y-y-you d-done w-with y-y-your g-g-g-golden arm?"

"YOU'VE GOT IT!"

And that's the last anyone's heard of Ray Jones.

BOO!

BY KEVIN CROSSLEY-HOLLAND

S HE DIDN'T LIKE IT AT ALL WHEN HER FATHER HAD TO GO DOWN TO LONDON, AND FOR THE FIRST TIME, SHE HAD TO SLEEP ALONE IN THE OLD HOUSE.

She went up to her bedroom early. She turned the key and locked the door. She latched the windows and drew the curtains. Then she peered inside her wardrobe and pulled open the bottom drawer of her clothespress; she got down on her knees and looked under the bed.

She undressed; she put on her nightdress.

She pulled back the heavy linen cover and climbed into bed. Not to read but to try to sleep—she wanted to sleep as soon as she could. She reached out and turned off the lamp.

"That's good," said a little voice. "Now we're safely locked in for the night."

ACKNOWLEDGMENTS

Grateful acknowledgment is made to the following authors, agents, and publishers for the use of copyrighted material. Every effort has been made to obtain permission to use previously published material. Any errors or omissions are unintentional.

"Taily-po" by Stephanie Calmenson. Copyright © 1991 by Stephanie Calmenson. Reprinted by permission of the author. Adapted from the story included in *The Book of Negro Folklore,* edited by Langston Hughes and Arna Bontemps, 1958. The story originated in Tennessee.

"Captain Murderer" by George Harland, published by Lothrop, Lee, and Shepard, 1986. This version has been adapted from the Charles Dickens story that was told to Dickens by his nurse when he was a young child. Dickens recorded it in *The Uncommercial Traveller.*

"Wait Till Martin Comes" from *The Thing at the Foot of the Bed and Other Scary Stories* by Maria Leach. Copyright © 1959 by Maria Leach, renewed in 1987 by Macdonald H. Leach. Reprinted by permission of Philomel Books. This is an adapted version of an African American folktale from the southeastern United States. In some versions the cat waits for Whalem-Balem instead of Martin.

"The Devil's Trick" from *Zlateh the Goat and Other Stories* by Isaac Bashevis Singer. Copyright © 1966 by Isaac Bashevis Singer. Reprinted by permission of HarperCollins Publishers. "The Devil's Trick" is a Central European Jewish legend.

"Little Buttercup" from *When the Lights Go Out: Twenty Scary Tales to Tell* by Margaret Read MacDonald. Copyright © 1988 by Margaret Read MacDonald. Reprinted by permission of the H. W. Wilson Company, New York. This story is based on the Norwegian folktale, called "Butterball," which is included in *Norwegian Folktales,* collected by the nineteenth-century folklorists Peter Christen Asbørnsen and Jørgen Moe, Pantheon Books, 1960.

" 'My Neighbor Is a Monster, Pass It On ' " by Eric Weiner. Copyright © 1993 by Eric Weiner.

"Bedtime Snacks" from *The Rainbow People* by Laurence Yep. Copyright © 1989 by Laurence Yep. Selection reprinted by permission of HarperCollins Publishers. This story is based on a Chinese American folktale. Tricksters such as Dagger Claws are popular in Asian storytelling.

"The Black Geese" from *Clever Gretchen and Other Forgotten Folktales* by Alison Lurie. Copyright © 1980 by Alison Lurie. Selection reprinted by permission of HarperCollins Publishers. This version of the folktale is an adaptation of "Baba Yaga's Geese." According to legend, the fearful Russian witch Baba Yaga rides through the air in a mortar or bowl and uses a broom to sweep away her tracks.

"Uninvited Ghosts" from *Uninvited Ghosts and Other Stories* by Penelope Lively. Copyright © 1974, 1977, 1981, 1984 by Penelope Lively. Reprinted by permission of Dutton Children's Books, a division of Penguin Books, USA, Inc. Certain words have been adapted from this British story with the author's approval.

"Duffy's Jacket" from *Things That Go Bump in the Night* by Bruce Coville. Copyright © 1989 by Bruce Coville. Reprinted by permission of the author.

"Good-bye, Miss Patterson" by Phyllis MacLennan. Copyright © 1972 by Phyllis MacLennan. The story originally appeared in *The Magazine of Fantasy and Science Fiction*, edited by Edward Ferman in 1972.

"The Witch Who Was Afraid of Witches" by Alice Low. Copyright © 1978 by Alice Low. Reprinted by permission of the author. The excerpt included in this book is from *The Witch Who Was Afraid of Witches*, a Harper Trophy Book, published by HarperCollins Publishers.

"Rap! Rap! Rap!" from *Witches, Wit, and a Werewolf* retold by Jeanne B. Hardendorff. Based on a story heard at Camp Conoy, Lusby, Maryland. Copyright © 1971 by Jeanne B. Hardendorff. Reprinted by permission of Curtis Brown Ltd.

"Boo!" from *British Folk Tales* by Kevin Crossley-Holland. Copyright © 1987 by Kevin Crossley-Holland. Reprinted by permission of Orchard Books, New York.

STORIES ADAPTED FOR THIS COLLECTION

"The Legend of Sleepy Hollow" retold by Della Rowland. Copyright © 1994 by Byron Preiss Visual Publications, Inc. This story is based on the classic tale written by Washington Irving. The Headless Horseman is a ghost who is said to haunt the residents of Tarrytown, New York. Many believe that the Headless Horseman exists today.

"Wiley and the Hairy Man" retold by Della Rowland. Copyright © 1994 by Byron Preiss Visual Publications, Inc. "Wiley and the Hairy Man" is based on the story recorded by Donnell Von de Voort in "Manuscripts of the Federal Writers' Project of the Works Progress Administration for the State of Alabama." The folktale was then published in *A Treasury of American Folklore* by B. S. Botkin. Copyright © 1944 by American Legacy Press.

"I'm Coming Up the Stairs" retold by Wendy Wax. Copyright © 1994 by Byron Preiss Visual Publications, Inc. "I'm Coming Up the Stairs" is a folktale that has been told by children to children in England, Canada, and the United States since the 1800s. A brief version that was told by a twelve-year-old girl in Alton, England, can be found in *Lore and Language of Schoolchildren* by Iona and Peter Opie. Copyright © 1959 by Oxford University Press, Ely House, London.

"The Strange Visitor" retold by Wendy Wax. Copyright © 1994 by Byron Preiss Visual Publications, Inc. "The Strange Visitor" is based on the folktale included in *English Fairy Tales* by Joseph Jacobs, published by the A. L. Burt Co., July 1, 1895. It also appeared in R. Chambers's *Popular Rhymes of Scotland*, 1890. Other versions of the story can be found in Walter De La Mare's *Animal Stories*, Elizabeth Hough Sechrist's *Heigh Ho for Halloween*, and Anabel Williams-Ellis's *Fairy Tales of the British Isles*.

"The Golden Arm" retold by Wendy Wax. Copyright © 1994 by Byron Preiss Visual Publications, Inc. The story is based on the folktale included in *English Fairy Tales* by Joseph Jacobs, first published by A. L. Burt Co., July 1, 1895. Another version of this folktale is called "The Golden Leg." Mark Twain also told his own version of this story, which can be found in *The Unabridged Mark Twain, Volume II* edited by Lawrence Teacher. Copyright © 1979 by Running Press, Philadelphia, Pennsylvania.